HARM'S WAY

A Horror Comedy

Marc Richard

This book is a work of fiction. Any resemblance to anyone you
know, whether they be alive or dead, is entirely in your head, and you
should probably seek help.

Dedication

This one goes o I dedicate this book to my friends and family. Of course I dedicate this book to my friends and family; who wouldn't? Biggest thanks goes out to my Jill. For everything. Thank you for making me believe. Ashaaabbadoobbabbbbadooshabbebabbabba.

.

Contents

1. The Horse

Jonesy stepped back a little from the sight that appeared in the back-yard before him. He ran his arm across his face to wipe the sweat from his bleary eyes. Was this really happening? A rainbow arced its way across the sky, but rather than the usual seven colors, it was a solid purple. A butterfly landed on his arm and pissed on it. Its left wing broke off and fluttered in the gentle breeze to land in the tall grass below his feet. It raised its right wing high in the air and took off, riding the wind like a lofty sailboat. The deer further toward the tree line laughed at this sight, somehow finding it all comical. It stood up on its hind legs and pointed a crooked finger at Jonesy.

"Deer don't have fingers... Deer don't have fingers... Deer don't have fingers..." he repeated over and over to himself like a mantra. And the more he repeated it, the more his legs drip-dripped until he sank into the puddle that they made around him. He was drowning in his own leg juice.

STOP!!!

He said to himself, and snapped out of it, a little, although the violet rainbow still hung stiff in the sky like a permanent stain in the atmosphere.

He didn't know why he took the acid; he hated the shit. Wait, it was all coming back to him now. He took it because his dad had run off with all of his heroin.

He went back indoors and re-read the note his father had left for him. The words were violently dancing across the page, but he was able to follow them around enough so he could read it again.

"Dear Jonesy, I went with Kim. Took your smack. Love you. Pops."

Who the fuck was Kim? She must be the new Taiwanese whore that he'd been seeing. That bitch! Not that he had a problem with his father running off with whores of any Asian descent, but she was obviously a junkie. His father didn't shoot heroin anymore, since he'd found his new drug of choice: vitamin C. Ever since he'd discovered it, he'd gone on and on and on about how great he felt, how healthy. How much energy he had. He'd tried to get Jonesy hooked on the stuff, but he didn't like the way it made him feel violently ill.

So damn his father, and damn the whore!

He gave his room another once-over, turning this thing over, moving that thing, running around like a crazed madman. Ever since he was three years old, man, all he'd ever wanted was heroin. The smack, the horse, the black tar, junk, H, Charley, poppy, Old Steve, chiva, Good and Plenty, etc., etc. He loved the stuff so much, he wanted to marry it, but George Bush wouldn't allow that sort of union. Marriage was between a man and a woman, case closed.

He restlessly ransacked the room. Needle, needle, needle, syringe. Nothing to put in them. Fuck! Fuck a duck! Wait. Duck. That's it! The duck! He raced to his closet, and there, in a little forgotten corner that still had his old duck wallpaper over it, behind the wall, was a little cubby. And there, in that little cubby, was his emergency stash. He'd had this stash for quite a while, and he wasn't sure if heroin aged well like a fine wine, or if it got old and rank like bad weed. Either way, it was junk, and junk was junk to a junkie like him. He contemplated using it right then and there. *No*, he thought. *I can hold out.* He would need this stash to take with him where he was going, but right now the remains of the acid in his bloodstream was not allowing him to remember just where that was.

The clock said 5:02. He was expecting something, he knew that much. But what?

RINGGGG RINGGGG! Went the fucking phone. Why did the phone always have to ring at a time like this? He was on the verge of a breakthrough. A thought was teetering in his head like a lonely suicide victim on the edge of a cliff. And now

RINGGGG RINGGGG!

and it's gone.

The clock said 5:04 now.

RINGGGG RINGGGG!

Will somebody shut that goddamned thing up? Why on earth did it make that terrible sound? To him it sounded like an ominous noise in a horror movie, one that was always meant to jump you, and then make you breathe a sigh of relief right before the real scare happened. Well he wasn't going to fall for its tricks.

Not this time.

RINGGGG RINGGGG!

5:07 now. 5:07 and it hadn't stopped for a full five minutes. It must have rung a hundred times or so. Why won't it stop?

RINGGGG RINGGGG!

"What!?!" he answered.

"Hey, Jonesy. It's Ben."

Ben, Ben, Ben. Who the fuck was Ben?

"Who?"

"Ben."

"I'm sorry, I..."

"Ben Smythe."

Silence.

"You have no idea who I am, do you?"

"Am I supposed to?"

"Uh, your buddy Ben."

Silence.

"Ben. We've gone to school together since the second grade Ben. You've been to my house to swim in my pool Ben. I'm inviting you to my cabin next week Ben."

"Ben. I'm sorry, man. I'm just tripping."

"Oh. I thought you were kidding around."

"No, I mean I am literally tripping right now, and I'm not enjoying it."

"Oh. Anyway, I was just calling to see if you were all psyched to go and shit."

"Oh yeah. Can't wait. Listen, Ben, can I call you tomorrow, if I ever come down from this? Right now I'm a little edgy."

"No need, my man. Just be ready Friday at 8 A.M. sharp. I'll be picking you up then."

He hung up, relieved. He was not in the mood for talking to anyone right now. Ben. Of course he knew Ben. He wasn't exactly what Jonesy would call a buddy, per se, but he supposed they were friendly enough that he could be considered a friend. But not a buddy. Jonesy had no buddies. So that's what he had planned. He was going to Ben's mother's cabin for ten days, with a bunch of other kids. A good way to spend a week, he supposed. Anything to get away from this hellhole.

Ben's cabin, here we come!

2. The Dark Child

I've been looking so long at these pictures of you, that I almost believe that they're real..."

She brushed the long pointy black hair away from her left eye. She was getting tired of brushing her long pointy black hair away from her left eye. She was wondering if she should spike it again. She was tired of being called "emo". She was not emo. She was postmodern goth, goddammit. Goth. Not emo. Emo kids listened to pop death metal garbage. She listened to beautiful music like The Cure, Skinny Puppy, and The Tear Garden. Emo kids were depressed because it was cool. Emo kids wrote the word "cool" this way: "Kewl" on their Facebook page. She was depressed because she was fucking born that way.

She lay in bed, one black nail tracing the faded line of some vague memory. She did these things to herself because she had to. Not because she wanted to. She doubted that anyone would ever really understand her, but what was the point in getting them to? She didn't need anyone. All she really needed was herself, and at this point in time, she wasn't sure she needed that.

The downy softness of the pillow contrasted too much with the heaviness of her thoughts. She must just let these images float away into nothing. Let it all dissolve into nothing. Let the words of Robert Smith wash it away and bring it down to nothing. Let it float downstream, tumble on the rocks, until little bits break off and they float, too. All gone. All away. All fine.

RINGGGG RINGGGG! RINGGGG RINGGGG!

Fuck!

"What?"

"Hey Kiera, it's Ben."

"Yeah."

"Ben Smythe."

"Yeah."

"From school."

"I know."

"I... just wanted to know if we were still on for this weekend," he stammered, obviously intimidated.

"Fuck."

"Uh, if you don't want to go, that's cool. I just thought it would be fun, you know. Camping and all that."

"I'll go."

"There's a bunch of us going; I think you'll have a good time."

"I said I'll go."

"You will?"

"Yeah."

"Okay, cool. 'Cause I think it would be nice to have you there. I just talked to Jonesy, and he's thrilled."

"Yeah. I gotta go. I'm right in the middle of Disintegration, and you're killing the mood."

"Okay, yeah sure. See you Friday."

"Right."

A face appeared in the doorway.

"Yes, Phyllis."

"Mom would be nice."

"Yes, mom."

"Honey, I was just wondering if you could turn that up."

Kiera just stared back at her mother blankly.

"What?" Phyllis said. "I like The Cure."

Getting out of bed with a heavy sigh, she hit the stop button and went over to her CD collection.

"What are you doing?"

"Tomorrow I'm burning all these fucking things."

3. The Southern Gentleman

Fllloyd! Ain't you finished all your chores yit?"

"Yes, paw!"

"Floyd! Where in sam-hell's your mama? Let her know to git her fat ass back in the kitchin! The chickin's sizzllin', and if she burns it this time, tomorrow night we'll be eatin' HER for dinnur!"

Floyd ignored that request. He was not about to go find his mama and tell her to get her fat ass back in the kitchen- not if he didn't want a two-by-four upside the head. He never sassed his mama, and he wasn't about to now- he was raised better than that. And besides, his mama never burnt anything in her life. Everything she made came out perfect, from her grits to her dumplin's to her peach pah. As far as he was concerned, she was the best cook in the world. She knew her job was to cook and clean the house, as all women were supposed to do, and she did it the best. Besides, he knew his paw wasn't serious or nothing. Floyd had noticed way too many empty red and white cans stacked up on the TV tray next to his paw's easy chair; he knew it was the beer talking.

RANGGGG RANGGGG!

RANGGGG RANGGGG!

"Hillo! Oh. Floyd! Pick up the goddamned phone! It's Baaayunnnn!"

Floyd rolled his three hundred pound frame off the bed with great effort, and trudged his way to the phone.

"Hey, Benny. How's it goin'?"

"Great. I just called Jonesy and Kiera, and they're both really excited about this coming week. What about you? Are you thrilled, or what?"

"Thrilled...? I...."

No, Floyd couldn't say he was particularly thrilled. Sure, it was nice to get out of the house once in a while, but he wasn't sure he wanted to hang out with all the people that were going to Ben's cabin.

See, the thing was, mama and paw one day decided to up and move clear up the country to Vermont. His paw got a chance to get a job transfer with a fifty-cent raise and took it. This was just three months ago. Floyd didn't really like it here. Moving to a blue state was like moving to a whole other country. Nobody said "Thank you, ma'am". Nobody had any respect for their elders. Nobody heard of the Bible here. Nobody watched rasslin'. Everybody's mama had a job outside of the house. And everyone was so open-minded here. There weren't many niggers in Vermont, and the niggers that did live here lived in perfect harmony with the white folks. Nobody even used the word "nigger" up here; they just called them "people". Sure, he supposed they were "people" in a way, but they were supposed to hang out with their own kind. And from what he gathered, there was one going on this trip. And that girl that wore black makeup. And that kid that was a little fancy in the pants. There was none of that where he was from. Sure, there were a lot of rough-and-tumble girls that he could have sworn had a hammer under their skirts, but for a boy to be gay, well that just didn't happen where he was from. It was like the north was a complete free-for-all, with everybody running around like a bunch of hippies, not caring about nothing. He just wished they'd stayed the hell in Georgia. Ben was okay, but he had made no other friends here, and he didn't know how he was ever gonna fit in.

"Goddammit, woman!" his father's voice came from the living room.

"Sorry, Benny. I gotta go. My paw done just threw a ree-mote control at my mama's head. See ya Friday."

4. The Death Pits of Rath

Whoosh! Wheeeeeeezzzz! Brent took a drag off his inhaler like it would be his last hit ever. He had thought about it one day, that if you killed him, took him to a lab, and ran him through various tests to determine his chemical composition, he would be at least ten percent albuterol. His allergies weren't acting up too badly today, but it was just a force of habit to keep the white plastic ell permanently attached to his lips at all times.

He did this all automatically, without notice. Right now he was enthralled, he was entranced, he was transfixed by the computer screen. He was playing Magic: The Gathering online, and he just laid down a card that would finally take out some top players, and seriously hurt others.

Or so he thought.

"Ohhhh, fungal-nuts," he said when he saw the card that had been laid down in response to his. This just negated everything he'd been working on up to this point. This ruined his plans to take over the game. Okay. Gotta think fast. The card that was laid down would kill a lot of the others. He had to prevent his own downfall. He had probably ten minutes to do so.

RINGGGG RINGGGG!

"Brent, honey. It's for you!" his mother shouted up to him.

"I'm busy," he shouted back down to her.

"Can't you stop playing that terrible game long enough to pick up the phone? It's Ben," she said, then added: "You're not still thinking of going on that camping trip, are you? What about your allergies?"

Rather than answering her, he picked up his extension. "Brent here," he said with authority, or so he thought.

"Yo, B-Dawg, what's up?"

"Huh?"

"What's going on?"

"Just playing Magic online."

"Oh. I was just calling to see if you were all set for Friday. I just talked to Jonesy, Kiera, and Floyd, and they can't wait."

"Oh, yeah. Listen, I don't think I can go. I got a lot happening right now. I've got Magic, and then there's a Kings of Chaos Tournament of Champions staring this weekend, oh, and I have to get my costume ready for my com-con-rom-com-com-com-dot-com-con, it's just not a good time for me right now."

"Brent. Dude. You gotta get your ass out of that chair, man. Get away from that computer for a while. I don't know what's happened to you, but ever since you started playing those games, I don't even see you anymore, outside of school. We really need to get together and, you know, reconnect," he knew he was spitting psychobabble at him, but he was hoping to come off as intellectual.

Brent thought about this for a second. He supposed he had been a little shut-off lately. He hadn't made himself easily accessible. And he liked Ben. "Yeah, you're right. But camping, I don't know..."

"Guy, you're killing me, here. Don't be a pansy."

"But will there be bugs?"

"Of course there'll be bugs, man. It's out in the middle of nowhere. That's all there is out there."

"Will there be wild animals?"

"Once again, Brent: Out in the middle of nowhere."

"Will there be pollen? Because my allergies, you know..."

"Of course there'll be pollen. That's all there is out there. Bugs, wild animals, and pollen. So are you in, or not?"

"Yeah, I guess so."

"It's not like we'll be roughing it. It's not exactly camping; it's my mother's cabin, for chrissake. Complete with electricity and running water and everything."

"All right, but will there be a crazed, deranged killer there, like in all of those scary movies?"

"Come on, Brent. Why would a crazed, deranged killer want to slaughter a bunch of kids in a cabin in the middle of nowhere? Ha-ha-ha-ha-ha."

"Ha-ha-ha. I guess you're right. I guess that's a ridiculous notion. There's no way on earth that that could ever happen."

"So I'll see you Friday."

"Yes, you will see me Friday."

"Cool."

He hung up the phone, and saw that he'd lost his turn and the game was now spiraling perilously out of control without him. He clicked the X at the top of the screen that would shut down Windows Explorer. Let them have their game; he was done.

5. The G

Jesus!

RINGGGG RINGGGG!

"Darnell, get the phone!"

"Shut up, bitch, I'm doin' it. Damn!"

"Don't you sass your mama, Darnell. Have you seen the bottom of my boot lately?"

"Yeah, it's black, dirty, and smelly, like yo' wack ass."

"Holla!"

"Hey, Darnell, it's Ben."

"Ay, Benny. What's happenin', playa?"

"Nothing. What are you up to?"

"Just tellin' my mama where to stick it."

"Oh, you mean yo' wack ass mama?"

"Don't ever talk like that about my mama, Ben. I ain't got shit to say about yours. Yet."

"Sorry. So what you been up to?"

"Shit, just doin' what I do. TWENTY-FOUR SEVEN."

"Did you just say Twenty-four seven?"

"That's right, Twenty-four seven."

"I'll keep that in mind. What else is up?"

"Oh you know, I gots my mind on my money and my money on my mizzind. My brother just went down to the sto' to get a fo-ty."

"That Snoop Dogg reference is from like twenty years ago. And why are you talking all ghetto today? You're from Vermont. And you don't even know what a forty is, do you?"

"It's forty ounces of malllltttt likkkkaaaaa, beeeyyyyaaattttcccchhhhh! Sorry about the ghetto talk. I'm just livin' the thug life."

"Thug life? Your parents run a maple syrup farm."

"That's right, bitch. Maple style."

"Whatever. So, are you still planning on going with us, or is your new black life going to interfere with your having fun? I called Jonesy and Kiera and Floyd and Brent already, and they're all looking forward to it."

"I don't know, my man. The black man doesn't go camping. The black man will not share in the simple man's recreation. The black man must rise above it all."

"Are you Farrakhan now?"

"My man, Farrakhan would be so lucky."

"Preach on."

"Right."

And Ben hung up, not knowing whether Darnell was going or not, but vowing to pick him up anyway.

6. The Deuce

RINGGGG RINGGGG!
"Hello?"
"Hello?"
"Hi, Uh, Muffy?"
"No, this is Buffy."
"Oh, hey Buffy."
"This is Muffy."
"Huh?"
"We're both on the line."
"Oh, you're on two phones."
"No."
"No."
"But how can that be?"
"What?"
"What?"
"How can that be that you're both on the phone?"
"Oh."
"Oh."

(Ben had never actually talked to them on the phone, only in person. Even though they were twins, somehow he could tell them apart. Buffy was the ugly one. He didn't know how or why, it was nothing he could put his finger on, but Muffy was the one he really wanted to bang. Buffy had the brains, though, so she was the one you'd want to marry.)

"So I'll make it short, because talking to you is making my head spin."

"Head spin, ha-ha, isn't that right, Muffy?"

"What did you say? Which twin am I talking to right now?"

"Me."

"Yes, but who's me?"

"Ben."

"But who are you?"

"I don't remember. Which one are you again?"

"Sometimes I forget."

"Sometimes she forgets, but there are times when neither one of us remembers shit."

"Yes, but which one are you?"

"The pretty one."

"That's not a nice thing to say about your own sister."

"What sister?"

"I don't know. So are both of you going to my camp still, or what?"

"What camp?"

"My mom's camp. You know, the one that's out in the middle of the woods."

"I don't know anything about that, do you?"

"Oh, yeah. I forgot to tell you, we're going camping."

"Okay. Yeah, Ben, I guess we're going camping."

"Good, because I already talked to Jonesy, Kiera, Floyd, Brent, and Darnell. And if you guys are definitely going, then there'll be EIGHT so far."

"Seven."

"What do you mean?"

"I changed my mind."

"Well, if she's not going, then I'm not going."

"Okay, I changed my mind back."

"Well, I'm still not going."

"Well, if she's not going, then I'm not going."

"I changed my mind back."

"Okay, so you're both going?"

In unison: "Yes, we are both going!"

"Oh, and bring your cousin Doris, too."

"Which one are you talking to?"

"Either. Don't you have the same cousin?"

"Not necessarily."

"Doris? Why should we bring him?"

"I don't know. The poor guy seems like he doesn't get out much; it might be good for him."

"All right, we'll bring the poor bastard."

"So I'll see you Friday."

"Yes."

"Oh, and somebody wants to say goodbye to you."

"Who's that?"

"Fluffy."

Sniff, sniff. Arf.

"Heh-heh-heh. Oh, Fluffy."

Poot.

7. The Faerie

He wept, knowing things were not right with the world.

RINGGGG! RINGGGG!

He put the phone next to his ear, his index finger knocking his toupee slightly askew. He readjusted.

"Hello?"

"Adam?"

"Hey you."

"What you doing?"

"Oh, just sitting here with a pint of Ben and Jerry's and a soup ladle. Oh, I wish this came in a gallon."

"What's wrong now?"

"Well, Celine Dion may only have three months to live."

"What are you talking about?"

"She has colorectal parasites."

"And where did you get this information?"

"The Enquirer. Where all the good news comes from."

"Adam, you are such a woman."

"How's that?"

"Caring that much about Celine Dion in the first place, and then believing what you read about her in the tabloids. Those two things make you either an old woman, or extremely gay."

"Well, you know damn well I'm not an old woman, Ben."

"I know. Listen, I'm sure Celine Dion is fine. And so are Bette Midler and Barbara Streisand, for that matter. You gotta stop believing everything you read when it comes to celebrities."

"Even Ashton and Demi?"

"Even Ashton and Demi," Ben said, not even calling him out on how dated that material was. "So I'll pick you up on Friday. Everybody else is all ready to go. And don't forget to bring your Elton John records. We can really get down to those."

"Ha-ha, very droll. I don't think I'm going to go."

"What??? You have to go. You're like one of my best friends. If you don't go I'll die."

"I think even if I do go you'll die. I get a bad vibe every time I think about going. I don't like the woods, Ben."

"Why not?"

"Well, there are wild animals out there, and I do not like that notion one bit, thank you."

"Now you're sounding like Brent."

"Like who?"

"Brent. You know Brent, a little nerdy."

"A little nerdy? Man, that kid makes the guys on that *Revenge of the Nerds* movie look cool."

"Hey, now."

"Well? And anyway, I don't really think I'm going to fit in with everyone else."

"What do you mean?"

"Let's be honest. You're the only one I've come out to. None of my other friends. No one in my family. Nobody else knows but you. But let's face it, everybody suspects it. Nobody wants a fag like me tagging along. I'll be ridiculed and humiliated."

"Do you even know who else is going? For Christ's sake. There's Darrell, he's the only black kid in Vermont. There's Jonesy the junkie. There's Brent the nerd. There's Floyd the redneck. There's Kiera the freak. And there's Muffy and Buffy, the twin whores. And their weird cousin Doris. And you think you won't fit in?"

"That's just my point. We're all typecast. It sounds like you're making a bad horror movie or something. In every one of those movies nowadays there's one of each. And now I'm the token queer."

"Adam, I invited all of those people because they're my friends. I just happen to have very diverse friends. You should be commending me for that, and not upset over it. And you just happen to be one of my best friends. And you just happen to be gay. I'm not inviting you to be the token. I'm inviting you 'cause you're my bud. And if you don't want to go, that's fine, but don't make it be because of your own hang-ups about yourself."

"Sigh. What time?"

"There's the Adam I know."

8. The Football Hero

Oh Chet, you're so suave, so debonair. Now tell me, how do you do what you do so well? You got all those little girlies under your spell. He gave the bathroom mirror a big kiss, leaving a smear of lipstick where his lips had been. That's our little secret.

He ventured back into his bedroom and gazed lovingly at all of the trophies he'd won, the three foot tall MVP trophy right up front, the track light glinting off the bronze helmet like a stationary disco ball. He was awesome. He was the best. He had never ever been laid, either, but that's another thing you and I will just keep to ourselves. He actually preferred the company of other men, and he got a thrill out of slapping the asses of his teammates out on the field, or snapping a wet towel over an unclothed naked boy-ass in the shower room. If the towel was really wet, it would leave a trace, a little trickle of water that would flow down and around the curves of the buttock, to be lost in the dark crease. But once again: Shhhh!

Oh, Chet, you are so cool. Right about now the phone is going to ring, and you will answer it, and it will be Ben, and he will say, "Hey Chet, camp will be so lame without you. Will you grace us with your presence?" And maybe you'll say yes, just maybe.

Ring, ring, man. His phone rang with a cool, laid back urgency.

"Hello," he said. No better way to greet someone than a cool hello.

"Hey Chet, it's Ben."

"Hey, sweetie... Petie... Ben. Hey Ben."

"So you going or what?" What a cool way to ask. Man, he was trying to out cool him. That was uncool.

"I don't know, maybe." Nothing cooler than being aloof.

"Just give me an answer, dipshit."

"Stop on by Friday and we'll see. If I get in the van, I'm going. If I don't, then you'll have to boogie without me."

Boogie? What was he saying? Boogie? Man, that word wasn't cool. He needed to think quick; his coolness was slipping.

"All right, but I'm sure you'll get in the van, as I'm sure you have nothing better to do."

"Oh yeah? Well, I beg to differ, my friend." Beg to differ? "Like...um, like..." Come on, man. Think of something. "Like watching paint dry." Oh, snap! That was good.

"Look, Chet, don't be lame, man."

Lame? Don't be lame? "You don't be lame, you lame-o. You lame-o homo fag."

Slammm!!!!

"Okay, Chet. Friday. Later."

Later? He couldn't let him leave with a "Later". That was about the coolest thing to say to someone when you were hanging up. Quick. To the point. Well, how about this?

"Lllll."

Oooh, cool. Click went the phone in the cradle. But wait, did Ben hang up before he heard that? He'd better call him back.

Ring, ring.

"Yes, Chet?"

"Lllll."

"I heard you the first t..."

Click.

Man, he was so cool he was emitting vapors. He laid on the bed and applied a ring of lipstick around the web of his hand. Tonight his fist was going to be the lovely Lady Chatterly. All aboard! The love train! Oooohh!

Marc Richard

Llllll.
Righteous.

9. The Mama's Boy

He put the receiver back in its cradle with a big sigh of relief. It was good to know that everybody was still going. He thought for sure that some of them would back out. Well, that was all well and good, but he wasn't out of the clear just yet. There was one big hurdle left. And here she comes now.

"NNNNOOOOOOOO!!!!" his mother shouted.

"What, ma?"

"You can't go to camp, Benjamin. You just can't go."

"Ma, you've been saying that for a month now, ever since I started planning this. You have yet to give me a reason."

"It's a den of sin."

"What's a den of sin? The camp? It's your camp."

"No, Ben. Not the camp. The whole situation. You inviting all of those other teenagers up there. You're setting yourselves up for very bad things to happen."

"What bad things, ma?"

"Well, like... like..."

"See? You can't even make me a valid point."

"Everyone will see your dirty pillows."

"Now you're just being childish."

"Bad things will happen, Ben, I can feel it."

"You're on crack. And what's all this about a 'den of sin'? You're not even religious."

"I mean that I know you are all going up there to do bad things. Drinking and smoking and having ess eee ex."

"Ma, we're just going up there to hang out. That's it. And so what if we were doing those things? We're not harming anybody."

"You're harming yourselves. Haven't you ever heard of karma? You do bad things, bad things will happen to you."

"That's ludicrous."

"I won't let you go."

"You can't stop me. That cabin is sitting up there doing absolutely nothing. You and I never even go anymore. It would be nice to get some use out of it. It could probably use a good cleaning out, anyway. Hey, tell you what. We'll spend the entire first full day there cleaning it for you. You know, throwing out the trash, sweeping, cleaning windows. You know how much you hate to clean windows."

She approached Ben with a look he hadn't seen in a while. Her head neared his neck and she gave it a soft, passionate kiss. "I'll tell you what," she said, her voice now a half-whisper. "How about you and I go. Just the two of us, just like the old days. Remember the fun we used to have up there, sweetie?" She moved in for a longer kiss, but Ben moved his head away.

He put his hand around her throat and held her up in the air. He got a deep satisfaction, as though he had been waiting for this moment for a long, long time. She was unable to fight back; he was so much bigger than she was, he could have killed her at this moment if he wanted. "Now listen to me and listen to me good. I'm going to the cabin this weekend. My friends are going to the cabin this weekend. We are going to have ourselves a good time, and I don't even want to think about you. And if you have the balls to stand in our way, woman, I'll mow you down quicker than shit. Do you understand me?"

His hold on her windpipe was too tight- she couldn't respond. The most she could do was nod her head, barely.

"Good," he said, and let her drop.

Her voice strained, almost breathless, she let out a squeaky, "I have a feeling..." pant, pant, "that..." pant, "I'll never see you again."

Not even sure what that meant, he shouted, "Arrgghhh!... Just...leave me alone!" and stormed out of the house. He needed air desperately.

"You'll be sorry," she tried to shout out the door at him, but couldn't say it loud enough for his ears.

"you'll be sorry..." again, to herself.

10. The Van

They were all packed in there like sardines, man. Ankles, chins, elbows, pelvises, fingers, tongues, rotator cuffs, teeth, hair, bone, blood, urine, and fecal matter. All piled one on top of the other so no one could tell where each began and ended. Ben had a feeling that when he stopped the van it would be impossible to separate them. He felt quite comfortable; he had the driver's seat all to himself, so despite the complaints, he was not inclined to stop for stretch breaks, pee breaks, etc.

They had been driving for what seemed like hours, but was probably more like hours. They had reached the end of civilization, or what passed for civilization in Vermont, and Ben knew from bitter experience that the 7-ELEVEN in St. Hockenberry was the very last stop before he had to make the long long trek down the long long boring road toward the Quebec border, where the camp was.

And there it loomed in the distance, like an oasis. And much like weary travelers that had crossed the great desert to get there, they were all parched and hungry. Ben himself could really go for one of those soggy prefab subs that they kept in the refrigerated case, right next to the cream cheese and jars of lemon curd. Slightly behind the pints of goat's milk and Trojan box that some discourteous traveler hadn't bothered to put back in its regular spot when he got an inkling that maybe he wasn't going to get lucky tonight after all. Maybe he was a loser with wishful thinking. And maybe he should have been nice enough to put the box of condoms on the back shelf, right next to the Ritz crackers and lantern batteries where he got them from. His rudeness and thoughtlessness was probably the reason he wasn't going to get laid in the first place.

Once they had all managed to un-Twister themselves out of the van, and stretch their muscles and re-set their joints back into place, they all walked together in a single line toward the store, strutting all cool-like, like in Reservoir Dogs. This scene would be much more effective if I could sell the movie rights to this story; instead I have to just try and describe it as best I can, and hope you know what I'm talking about.

And into the store they walked, having an air about them of teenage greed and horniness, with a bitter aftertaste of mildew.

"Hello, my friends! Welcome to 7-11!" The overzealous cashier said, a little too zealously.

Not one of them returning his greeting, they all got busy picking out what they were going to get. The back of the van was already loaded with enough groceries to feed three battalions for three months, but they needed something to sustain them for the next three hours that it would take them to get there.

Ben got a Snickers bar, a bag of chips, and a Coke.

Adam got a pint of Cherry Garcia, of course.

Muffy and Buffy got a pack of Doublemint gum (how cute).

Darnell got a bag of Doritos and a pint of strawberry milk.

Brent got a tube of Pringles and a box of Nerds.

Kiera got a Slim Jim and a diet cola.

Jonesy got the munchies from the weed he had smoked before he left the house two hours ago, much to his dismay, and had his arms full.

Floyd got a bag of jerky and a copy of TV Guide.

Doris got nothing, for he was still in the van. He had gotten his guitar out from the back and was happily strumming "Patience" by Guns N' Roses.

"Hey, just where do you think you're going with those, Chet? You're not TWENTY-ONE." Brent asked, indicating the two cases of beer he was carrying.

"Shhh."

"Well, I don't know if I like this very much," Brent squeaked.

"Hey man, stop being so square. Don't you want beer?"

"I...well...How are you going to purchase those?"

"With money, stupid. What's it going to take to get you to shut up?"

"I don't know...I..."

"What do you want? Anything, just shut up."

"I need Sudafed."

"Sudafed? I say I'll get you anything you want, and you say, 'Sudafed'?"

"My allergies are going to be really bad, I can tell already. And my prescriptions are weak. And you have to be eighteen to buy Sudafed, and since you're already breaking the law..."

"All right, fine. I'll tell you what. I'll get you a lottery ticket, too. Go fill out a Megabucks card."

"Really?"

"Yeah. You gotta be cool, and you can't be cool unless you gamble and drink, man. So you can at least gamble."

So off he went to fill out the card. Man, it was just like taking his SAT's. He thought for a minute, and then filled out numbers that were significant to him. He didn't just want the easy pick. One by one he filled in the numbers, THIRTEEN, EIGHTEEN, THIRTY-TWO, SIXTEEN, THIRTY-FIVE, THIRTY-NINE. He brought it to Chet and watched him work his magic.

Chet slammed the beer on the counter in front of the Middle Eastern dude, rattling the Zippo display and almost knocking it over.

"Yes, my friend, can I help you?" the clerk asked helpfully.

"Just the beer, man. Oh, and this," he said, and handed him Brent's ticket. "Oh, and some Sudafed. Oh, and a pack of Winstons."

"May I see some identification?"

"Don't I look twenty-one?"

"No, I'm afraid not. I am very sorry, but if you do not have identification, I cannot sell you these things."

"Aw, come on, Habib."

"Look at my name tag. Does it say 'Habib'?"

He did. It said "Hank".

"I do not call every American John, why do they insist on calling me Habib?"

"My apologies, Hank."

"Once again, I am very sorry."

"Oh, you're going to be," Chet said, as he pulled a handgun out of the waistband of his underwear, which was actually not a handgun at all, but rather a very nice replica fashioned out of a block of processed cheddar cheese, the authenticity betrayed only by the fact that it was bright orange, and it was so old that it had grown quite funky.

Not even caring about the fact that it was obviously a sham, Hank reached down behind the counter and pulled out his very real shotgun. "You do not do this. You do not do this," he explained to Chet.

"Woah, woah, okay. Hey, calm down, man. It's just cheese. See?" he said, and took a bite of the stinky food. "Hey, I was just trying to have some fun. I'd never pull a real gun on you. Gee, I'm awfully sorry about that. It's just, we're going to camp, and we just wanted to have some fun, you know? Figured we could get some beer. And my friend here's really sick, and he really needs the Sudafed and cigarettes and lottery ticket. I could have had a fake ID made, but I'm much too honest for that."

"My friend," Hank said, "in my country, we have a saying. An honest man is like a hive of angry bees. Of course I will sell you these things; your honesty humbles me. Get a few more cases, if you'd like. It's on me."

So out the store and back in the van they went. "Said woman, take it slow," Jonesy sang. Man, that Doris cat could really play that thing.

11. The Old Dirt Road

They sang so off-key, but it didn't matter.

"TWENTY-TWO bottles of beer on the wall.

Twenty-two bottles of beer.

Take one down, pass it around, twenty-one bottles of beer on the wall."

"And one more in our bellies," Muffy insisted on saying at the end of every verse. They were all the way down to fifteen bottles, and if it was annoying at 100, it was presently like a bowling ball being dropped on your face after a multiple tooth root canal. And then getting a paper cut on your ass.

But nobody said anything, because:

A: They all wanted to be polite

B: They were all too busy singing the rest of the song, and

C: They all wanted a piece of her, except for Adam and Kiera, and maybe Doris (but Ben wouldn't put money on it).

The way to the camp was a very confusing labyrinth of back roads and dirt paths through the thick Vermont forest. They had last seen pavement about an hour ago. Ben had taken the turn onto Clover Street, drove approximately ten more miles to where the tarmac ended abruptly and dumped them out onto the dirt road. There was always this bump in the road, way back as far as he could remember, as well as potholes the entire length, and he was unsure why they didn't just fix it. There was still a fair amount of traffic on this particular road, and he'd always thought that if they couldn't spend tax money to pave it, the least they could do was fix that damned bump.

That road was called, ironically enough, Macadam Way, and it was fairly populated. There were still houses lining both sides of the street, some of them fairly nice, as though people had harbored the hope that some day they too would become a part of civilization.

But as the miles went on, the dwellings got fewer and farther between, until there were barely any at all. The road forked, with Macadam continuing on to the left, and another, slightly narrower one going off to the right. This was Crooked Brook road. He took it.

Ben had come here with his mother annually, sometimes four or five times a year, so he knew the roads like the back of his hand.

It occurred to him now that he only had a vague idea of what the back of his hand looked like, and that maybe he should study it more often, because he was growing more and more aware that he quite possibly had no idea where they were. None of this was looking right to him at all. Miles ago, he'd thought he saw a tree at the side of the road that seemed familiar, but that was miles ago, and now he seemed lost.

"It doesn't make sense, guys. I know I was supposed to take the right onto Crooked Brook, go ten miles, take a left, go another five, veer left, then take a right through the narrow path until I got to the road we're on now, and it should seem right, but it doesn't. None of it looks right to me. We're lost. Lost and doomed."

He said none of this. And he was hoping that the look of despair that he knew damn well was on his face right now spoke nothing of how lost and disoriented he felt.

You know, it was the funniest thing. This road was narrow enough that if you were to meet another car coming the opposite direction, you would have to pull over into the ditch to pass by each other successfully. And now, in the distance, he could swear there was an eighteen-wheeler barreling right for them.

"Uh," Darnell piped up. "Ben, is that an eighteen wheeler barreling right for us?" Darnell didn't use hyphens. They were the white man's punctuation.

"Mmmm, I think so," he answered.

"Why would there be an eighteen wheeler on this road?"

"I don't know," he answered.

"I don't see a place to pull over, man. What are you going to do?"

"Shh, let me think," he answered.

There were only two options: One was to drive forward as fast as he could, and hope he found a place to pull over up ahead. The other was to back up and do the same thing.

Not taking much time to think, he slammed the car in reverse and stepped on the gas as hard as possible. He did not like driving backwards this quickly, especially when he couldn't see out the back window. They were all going to die.

"Hurryup, Benny. We're gonna dah!" Floyd shouted, as he watched the tractor trailer get quickly closer and closer.

Ben chanced a look forward and estimated that he probably had about fifteen more seconds before they were all flattened like a stack of johnnycakes. He looked back in the side-view mirror and swerved slightly. *Oh God, don't start fishtailing,* he prayed, and got the big van under control.

"Why isn't he stopping?" Adam pleaded.

"Aaaahhh!!!!" most of them screamed as Ben jerked the wheel to the right hard, and flew into the small clearing in the trees as the semi bore down on them, just barely squeaking by.

"Holy shit," Jonesy exclaimed. "That truck was doing eighty, if it was doing a mile."

"Is everyone okay?" Ben asked the back seat.

"Yeah," most of them replied.

"I think I just shit myself," Adam confessed.

"Uh, guys..." Brent started. "Did anyone happen to get a look at the driver?"

None of them had.

"I...uh...I looked in the driver's window when it passed by..."

"Yeah?" Kiera said.

"I...uh...I don't think there was a driver."

"Okay, is everybody ready to roll?" Ben asked, and didn't wait for a response; dark was approaching all too quickly, and he still had no idea where they were.

But he did when, ten minutes later, he passed the little concrete building owned by a phone company that was silly enough to provide service in this area.

So they were on the right road, after all. There was no possible way that there were more than one of these buildings in this area.

And what was that Buick Skylark doing parked there?

"What are you doing?" Kiera asked, as Ben pulled the van to the side of the road.

"There's something weird here," Ben explained.

"It's just a car," Kiera said. "Can't a car park where a car wants to park?"

"Maybe it's someone from the phone company," Jonesy said.

"Maybe somebody broke down," Brent said.

Kiera nudged him. "I'd like to get to camp sometime today," she whispered.

"Broke down in this exact spot?" Ben said. "And I don't think it's the phone company, either, out here so late. No, something's not sitting right with me."

He got out of the van, slowly approached the car, and puked instantly when he looked in the car's rear window.

"What?"

"What is it?"

"What is the sight you see that is making you vomit so?"

One by one they got out of the van, and one by one they approached the morbid scene, and one by one they vomited. Chunder flew forth in every direction, out of the mouths of all, and out of the noses of most. Adam threw up so hard that a vile green fluid leaked from his eye sockets, and his hairpiece ejected itself from his scalp and landed in a puddle of his own stomach juices. He picked it up, wiped it off, and put it back on his very own hairy head. He didn't care how sick he was; there was no way in hell he was leaving his toupee.

They had all seen horror movies, and they had all witnessed gruesome sights in those movies, but this sight here had more grue than all of those movies put together. No screenwriter on earth had ever thought to put this scene together.

The two young lovers had obviously pulled over to get themselves involved in a steamy bit of romance.

And whoever slaughtered them had caught them in the middle of it.

And didn't just kill them, but butchered them. Butchered them in a fashion that should never be described in words.

But what the hell...

The girl must have been in the midst of fellatio, as the boy's penis was still in her mouth, detached, the blood that had obviously been dripping from the sliced end of it now crusted and flaky on her chin. She had been stripped completely nude, whether by her boyfriend or the killer was unclear, and her nipples had been cut off and inserted in the boy's open eyes, like fleshy contact lenses. The boy's testicles had also been removed and stuffed in his anal cavity, although none of the kids knew that. All they knew was that there were two balls unaccounted for. The boy's fist had been rammed up inside the girl's vagina; the severed bloody wrist enveloped in the folds of her labia, being the only thing visible, was crawling with flies.

The entire interior of the car was covered in blood. Ben didn't think it was possible for two human beings to emit this much blood. He had to go. They had to get out of here.

"Well, everybody ready?"

"Ready for what?" Brent asked.

"To get going. We still have to make camp before nightfall, or we're all screwed."

"Yeah, let's get out of here," Jonesy agreed. "This scene's really getting me down."

And one by one they all piled back in the van, except for Doris, who never left the van in the first place, but had gotten his guitar out and was happily strumming "Dust in the Wind".

"Wait a minute," Chet said, "I have a feeling," and approached the car once more.

"What are you doing?" Ben asked.

"You'll see," he said. He opened the driver's side door, and took the bloody key out of the ignition. He walked around to the back of the Skylark, put the key in the trunk, and opened it.

"What the fuck?" Ben said, and everybody turned their heads at once, as though they all expected to see more gore.

"Aha! Just as I thought! Look!" Chet said, and they all collectively turned their heads back out their windows.

Chet held the case of beer up in his hands like a trophy. "I can always tell when there's beer," he shouted to the others. "I can smell a beer can like a hound dog can smell a rabbit!"

Darnell clapped, slowly. And, one at a time, they all joined him, until Chet was receiving a very nice round of applause.

'Cause dead is dead, but free beer is free beer.

12. The Visitor

Ben was elated when he was finally driving down the road that his camp was on. He beamed when he caught a glimpse of the sign:
HARM'S WAY

The sign had looked like this for years. As he remembered, it used to be called "HARMON'S WAY", named after one of the families that used to live here. Some jokester had removed the ON shortly after...well...

Ah yes, Harm's Way, the long and winding road that led to the camp. It was a five mile trip or so just to go down that road. His camp was the only one inhabited on that road. There were three other houses on the way to his camp, but nobody lived there now. Not since the incidents.

Ben remembered hearing the stories when he was younger. Each house had a different tale, each occurring at a different time, but each story was essentially the same.

As they drove past, he recalled them. House number one, on the left hand side of the road. A quiet little white ranch. The Harmon family. A Brady Bunch family if ever there was one, a blended family with get this: Nine children. How they all fit in a quiet little ranch is not relevant here. What is relevant, however, is that they were all dead. House number two, a nice big cape on the right. The Dunwoodys. These were the only people on the street that Ben got the chance to meet. They seemed nice enough, but the kids were just weird. Ben had an idea that this was their house, not their camp, as they were always there. Here they lived, two million miles from any schools their kids should have been going to, and two squillion miles from civilization in general. And one day, about six years ago, the parents, the husband's mother, their cousin Bob, their other cousin Junior, and their six kids, all got slaughtered. Ben remembered that day well. It was two days before he and his mom had planned to come up. Despite much protesting from Ben, his mom, Allison Baconhammer Smythe, decided they would just stay home that year. And then there was the little trailer, also on the right, and not half a mile from Ben's camp. This was the third group to be slayed. Eleven kids, all staying in that one tiny camp one year. He didn't even think any of them owned the place. They were all also murdered.

They never did catch the killer. I use the singular term because it was obvious, with the methods used, and the amount of creativity involved, that it was all the same person.

Yes, there were four houses on the road. Four houses, and his was the only one left untouched. His was the only one without police tape around it. The killings didn't happen so long ago that they couldn't happen again, but somehow he never felt scared, in all the times of coming up here. He felt somehow protected. Nothing bad could happen here; he just knew it. He knew it as well as he knew the roads that led here.

"What's with all the police tape?" Adam asked.

"Oh," said Ben, reciting a speech he had practiced, since he knew he would be asked, "those camps haven't been lived in for years. Nobody has ever come up here to take care of any of them, and they have all fallen into such states of disrepair that the town passed an ordinance to get them all condemned. They held a meeting and everything, and since nobody showed up to defend the houses, they just went ahead and taped them all up." He felt he was being too verbose- that he was coming across as over-explaining the situation, so he thought he would just shut up at that point. Lucky for him, there were no more questions about it.

He checked the clock as they pulled into his driveway. 9:27. Not too bad. Getting lost only put them a half-hour or so behind his prediction.

The funny thing about NINE THIRTY at this time of year was that it wasn't light out by any means, but there was still enough twilight to make it optically tricky.

Though he could only partially make it out, he didn't need to see it to know how beautiful the place was. A cape, about the same size as the one up the road, but with an addition that had been built shortly after Ben was born. The camp was well taken care of; they would never let it fall into disrepair as many of the other camps around the area had been. Ben's mother paid to have the camp painted professionally two years ago, and it really made the place look brand new. It used to be light blue in color, now royal blue. The front door was fire engine red. There were three steps leading up to a porch that Allison had built in front of the addition five years ago. The tiny lawn had become slightly overgrown by now, of course, but he made sure it was nice and well-kept when he was there. That was one of the first things on his to-do list: Mow the lawn.

As he led his fellow travelers to the camp, everything became so familiar to him once again. He almost allowed himself to forget the sights, sounds and smells of the place, but every time he came here, the sensations were the same, and here they were again: The smell of the pine trees bordering the yard, the sound of the crickets and peep frogs chirp-chirp-chirping, the crunch of the gravel driveway that led to the house. And the sights, as he came upon them: The little fence on the right of the driveway that his mother had put up to protect her little herb garden, the basketball hoop, the maple tree in the front yard, the dead virgin skewered on the newel post.

The dead virgin skewered on the newel post? He didn't remember that being there before. Maybe his eyes were playing the twilight trick.

But when he led the crew closer to the house, he discovered that that was indeed what it was: A dead, naked virgin skewered on the newel post. "Aaaahhh!!!!" The ladies and Adam screamed as they approached her. Ben wanted to look away, but he couldn't. There she was, totally nude, with the newel post of the banister shoved in her crotch. A girl of about sixteen, and one he didn't recognize. It was obvious that she was dead because she wasn't moving or breathing. It was obvious she was a virgin, or at least a virgin to newel posts, because the post wasn't that large, and the impact it had when she was shoved upon it was horrid. It split her wide open, the gash going all the way to her belly button. There was no telling if this was what killed her, but there were no other signs of injury, as far as he could tell. It was also obvious that she hadn't been dead for long, as decay had yet to really set in, and there were very few flies buzzing around just yet.

"Look away," he told the others, and as he led them into the house, the men were nice enough to shield the ladies' eyes. Jonesy had Kiera's head buried in his chest as he made his way up the steps; Chet had Muffy and Buffy both taken care of, and Darnell covered Adam's eyes with his hand, telling him when to step up.

They all got inside safely, but Doris was still in the van. He had his electric guitar out now and was playing Hendrix's version of "The Star Spangled Banner".

"Doris, are you coming?" Brent shouted out the window.

Reluctantly, Doris grabbed his guitar and his little battery-powered amp and wandered inside.

"What's up?" he said to the dead virgin, and stepped into the porch and then the house, letting the door slam.

"Don't let the door slam again, Doris. My mother's knickknacks like to fall off the shelves," said Ben, but he was talking to thin air. Doris had already found the bedroom he wanted upstairs, and was in there, playing his stupid guitar.

13. The Confession

All were safely indoors. And most of the eyes were turned toward Ben.

Muffy's heavy breaths became blankets. Steam rose from her shattered eyebrows. She was ready to break. Suddenly, without warning, she climbed onto the table, like an old lady frightened of a mouse scampering around on the linoleum kitchen floor.

"What was that?!?!?" "What the fuck was that?!?!?" "Where am I? Huh? What are you doing to us, you sick bastard?" Is this your idea of a joke? Because I'm not laughing. It's not funny. IT'S NOT FUNNY! WAS THAT REAL? WAS THAT EVEN REAL? WHAT THE FUCK? ANSWER ME! SHE WAS REAL, WASN'T SHE? OH MY FUCKING GOD OH MY GOD OH MY GOD!!! THIS IS NOT RIGHT! NONE OF THIS IS RIGHT! WHERE AM I? WHERE ARE WE? WHERE

are

we?"

She said, and fell backward. Caught in the nick of time by Super Chet, of course.

"Any time, lady," he said to her, but he was being a total douche bag, because she couldn't hear a thing.

"The fuck's that bitch's problem?" Darnell quipped.

Kiera turned from the standing-on-the-table fiasco back to Ben, her eyes so fierce with evil wishes they were melting little sausage-shaped holes through his brain. "You're an asshole, Ben," she said, and didn't leave him any room for rebuttal.

"Wha..." he said, but it was too late, for she had already gone up into Doris' room and slammed the door.

"What did I do?" he shouted upstairs, and then directed the question toward Brent, who only shrugged.

"Don't worry about that bitch, man. Dey all wack."

"For fuck sake, Darnell, would you stop talking like that?"

"Like what?"

"What you got to eat?" Floyd, who had his nose buried deep in the refrigerator, disgusted by the fact that there was nothing in there but a box of baking soda and an old egg, interrupted.

"Man, this is too much for me. See you in the morning," Jonesy said, grabbing his bag and taking it downstairs to one of the bedrooms in the basement and shutting the door.

"You guys don't think I had anything to do with this, do you?" he asked the rest of the gang that was still present and conscious.

Darnell walked up to Ben, and affectionately touched his shoulder. "You're all right, Ben. You're all right," and walked away.

Was that any sort of answer to his question?

He approached Adam. "You don't think I had anything to do with this, do you?"

Adam twisted his head from side to side, a gesture that generally means no in most cultures. "I know you better than that, Ben. But who is that girl?"

"I have no idea," he said. "Come on, let's take another look."

"I don't know if I..."

"I need to talk to you in private, dude."

"Oh, okay," Adam said, and was led out to the porch.

He faced away from the girl as Ben talked to him. He just didn't have the stomach for things like that.

"Listen, man, I've got something to tell you, but you can't tell anybody else, okay?"

"Yeah, sure. Whatever you say, man. You know me. Zip it and skip it."

"Right. Well. I guess I wasn't up front with you about what's happened here in the past."

"What do you mean?"

"Those other camps on this road- the ones that are all taped up- those weren't just allowed to fall into disrepair."

"I thought that was odd, that it happened to all three of them," Adam said.

"You see, the thing is, the people in the camps were all...well...slaughtered."

"Slaughtered?"

"Yeah, slaughtered. And all apparently by the same killer. And it wasn't all that long ago. They all happened years apart, but they all happened in my lifetime. The Harmons owned the first camp. They were all butchered. The Dunwoodys lived in the second. They got theirs. And the camp next to this one, it was a group of teenagers that got dead."

"Wow."

"One camp right after the other, man. Eleven people each time."

"Wow."

"And they never caught the killer."

"Wow."

"And this camp is the next one in line, and the only one left."

"Wow."

"And we're a group of eleven."

"Wow."

"And now we come here, and there's some random dead girl on my porch. And she hasn't been dead long- maybe a day. It's almost as though the killer knew we were coming. As though he'd been waiting for this chance for a long, long time."

"Wow. Well, that's quite a story, Ben."

"You don't believe me?"

"That's quite a story."

"I can't believe you don't believe me. You, who believes everything he reads in the tabloids. You, who has a conspiracy theory for everything. For fuck sake, man, you think that the reason you can't get a full bowl of cereal when you get down to the end of the box is not due to miscalculations on your part, but has something to do with the CIA."

"I don't believe that anymore, Ben."

"But you won't believe me, either. Why else do you think that dead girl's here?"

"I don't know. Maybe she put herself there, you know, for pleasure purposes, and got in over her head."

"Then where did she come from? Huh? Answer that. And why would she come here? To my place? None of it makes sense. The only way it makes sense is if you believe what I just told you. Adam, look at me."

He did, and his expression changed. He saw the sincerity in Ben's eyes.

"You know I wouldn't lie to you. I've known you my whole life. Neither one of us hides anything, you know that. Hell, I know you better than I know myself. And you should know me better than to think I would make something like that up."

"You're right," Adam said. "I'm sorry. Still friends?"

Ben put his arm around Adam's shoulder. "Stupid question. Now come on, they're probably all wondering where in the hell we went," he said, and led Adam inside.

When they walked through the door, Ben's arm still around Adam's shoulder, they were greeted by Floyd, who had in his hand the largest turkey leg Ben had ever seen.

"What wurr you gahs up to?" Floyd asked, the leg dripping fatty deposits on the living room carpet.

"Nothing. And none of your fucking business. And where in the hell did you get that turkey leg?"

"Oh," Floyd said, grinning. "A Georgia boy has his ways."

14. The Rest

He put the syringe into the dissolved mixture and sucked it all up. He stuck the needle in his arm, withdrew the plunger a bit (At this point in the game, this practice was no longer necessary. He knew blood would flow into the syringe, because he knew every vein in his body like he knew the back of his hand, which he also occasionally injected into), and went for the gold. The white gold, red chicken, hell dust, joy powder, number FOUR, old Steve.

This was it. The last of the load. The finale of the foo foo. The completion of the carga. His original intent was to make it last. He'd brought enough for two moderate doses, and he could have spaced them out enough during the week that he wouldn't have gotten the shakes, and then he could be fine until he made it home and confronted his father, were he to ever return from his sordid affair with the Laotian woman or whoever she was, hopefully bringing the remainder of the smack that she didn't end up consuming back home with him, and paying Jonesy for the stolen stash. He could have made it that long, if he were wise. And he could have saved his pokes for nights when they were really having a good time here. Not for dodging reality. That's how most addictions started- not because you were taking the drugs for fun, but because you wanted to escape. Jonesy never needed the drug to escape; he always used it for fun. Therefore, he was not an addict. *I may have to reassess that today,* he thought, as he injected all of what he had left into his arm.

But who wouldn't want to escape from what had just happened? He would bet anything that Doris was still playing his guitar, Floyd was gnawing on a turkey leg, Chet was guzzling beers, Adam was eyeball deep in Star magazine, et cetera, et cetera. They were all escaping. I mean, this situation they had now gotten themselves into was fucked up. Something was rotten in Denmark, and...

and...

The warm fluid made its way up from his arm and quickly spread to his entire body. Good place. Good place. His mind was in a good place. Wha?

What was he thinking about before the warmth? Something out there. The other kids were doing something. What? Was he supposed to be out there? Man, forget it. Forget thinking. He didn't need to think anymore. If it was that important, he could think about it later. Right now, just let your mind become blank, Jonesy. Put on the tunes, sink into the carpet, and enjoy the ride. Buenas noches.

15. The Big Let Down

Say," Ben began, "who knows how to play Parcheesi? Or I have a cribbage board here. We could get a nice tournament going. Maybe some poker? I'll put a few beers in the freezer and they should be cold before too long."

"I don't know," Buffy said. "I think I'll pass. I need to look after her," she said, gesturing at her sister. "Make sure she's all right."

"Understood," Ben agreed. "So, who's ready to play?" Ben asked. He looked at Brent, whom he knew was a master at any game, adventure or otherwise. "Come on, man. I'll kick your ass in cribbage."

"I don't know, I'm kinda tired. It was a long ride and all, and my asthma's really bad already. I think I'll retire early. Get a nice night's sleep, and then I'll be up for anything. Goodnight, all."

"Goodnight," they all answered in unison.

"Where you sleeping?" Ben asked.

"What are the options?"

"Well, there's Jonesy's room and another room downstairs, and there's one bedroom left upstairs. I guess Kiera and Doris have already decided to shack up."

"Ooooh!" said the mob.

"And I got the master bedroom, so don't even think about it. My house, my rules."

"Right, well, guess I'll sleep downstairs," Brent said.

"I'm right behind you," Adam said.

"All right, Adam, but I'll let you know I talk in my sleep," Brent informed him.

"I'll let you know he likes dudes," Chet answered in response.

"Chet, shut the fuck up," Ben said. "Okay, two more down. Any takers on some fun tonight?"

"Count me out," Darnell said. "I'm beat, man. Way too much excitement for me. Tomorrow we'll wake up, decide what we're going to do with the dead chick, and we'll all gather wood or something or kill deer or whatever it is you crackers do. Later."

Faintly, heard from downstairs: "Hey Jonesy, what you... Woah, man. Hey, you got anymore of that?"

Ben turned to Chet. "So I guess you're tired, too, huh?"

"Well, yeah, I guess I could use some shuteye," he said, and grabbed a warm beer from the counter. He turned to Floyd. "Guess it's you and me, buddy."

"Good enough," Floyd answered, and they both headed upstairs.

"Goodnight, guys," Ben said to their backs.

"Well," he turned to Buffy. "Guess you guys have had your spot picked for you. You probably shouldn't move her too much anyway."

Ben helped Buffy fold out the sleeper sofa and put sheets on it. Muffy was put to bed, and Ben bid them goodnight.

"Guess I better get some sleep too. See you in the morning."

16. The Thing Nobody Needs to See

Aaaaahhhggggggrgggrrrgggg!

"Huh? What the..." Ben said, erupting forth from his dream.

"Aaahhhgrgrgggggaaawwww!"

The sound perhaps ranked among the top ten blood-curdling screams in the history of blood-curdling screams. A girl's scream; it had to have been one of the three girls. It was soon followed by several very loud bangs that shook the floor, slightly. Well, he was certainly no superhero, but he was no coward, either. Arming himself with the first thing that he could get his hands on, which just happened to be an issue of TV Guide from three years ago, he fled out of his room and down the short hallway at full speed.

Bang! Bang! Bang!

He threw open the guest room door and suddenly felt very peculiar. He didn't like this feeling at all. He felt as though ants were marching their way through his nervous system and were eating the picnic lunch he had stored in his spinal cord.

Doris was over by the bed, guitar neck in hand, smashing, smashing, smashing it onto the hardwood floor. This wasn't Kurt Cobain style, either. This wasn't I'm going to show how antisocial I am by showing how I could care less about the business that I make my living doing, and destroying my equipment. This was pure anger. Doris had a look in his eye that said, There is a devil in this instrument, and goddammit I will beat it out.

Ben watched this spectacle until there was nothing left in Doris' hands but the headstock and a few dangling strings. His attention turned then to Kiera, who appeared to be fine, except for the fact that she was standing in the middle of the floor absolutely motionless, absorbing none of this fiasco, just staring at the doorway. She had been doing this since Ben came in, and although she looked all right, there was something about the look on her face that said otherwise.

He walked around her until they were face to face. Although she was looking right at him, her eyes did not register him at all. Perhaps she was sleeping.

"Kiera?" he dared ask.

Finally, her eyes focused and saw Ben, but now they looked baffled. "Kiera?" she repeated.

Arrhhhgghhheeeaaaaaaaa! The scream once gain issued forth from Kiera, but this was no longer a girl's scream. This was an inhuman scream. This was the scream of the pits of hell. This was the scream of millions of years of millions of tortured souls condensed into one sound.

Smoke escaped from every orifice in her face, and her eyes caught fire. Soon her entire face was engulfed in a maddening frenzy of flames. The scream continued ceaselessly.

"Aaaarrhhgggheghee-hee-hee!"

"Huh? What the..." Ben said, erupting forth from his dream.

"Arrhhgggerrrrr!"

The sound didn't really rank in the list of blood-curdling screams. It wasn't scary enough to curdle his blood, but it was enough to cause a twitching in his lower digestive tract that began in his duodenum and stopped somewhere around his semicolon. He had to poop, but he could hold it. This noise was coming from downstairs. It sounded like someone was being murdered, but in a friendly fashion. Now there were two screams- screams that said, I'm dying, here, but I'm having fun doing it. Well, lest he be called a candyass, he grabbed the first thing that he saw, which appropriately just so happened to be a Louisville Slugger, and headed downstairs. Those poor girls had been through enough already tonight, but to be murdered on top of everything else? He could not let that happen. He marched down the last few steps, ready to beat the brains out of whomever was torturing the twins.

But it was no killer that greeted him at the bottom of the stairs.

No, no. This was far worse.

This was a sight that would take him a lifetime of alcoholism and years of psychotherapy to erase even a trace of from his damaged mind.

There was Chet, in Muffy and Buffy's bed, completely unclothed, the moonlight shining off his pale ass, his weasel-like penis flouncing back and forth as though it were doing jumping jacks, as he moved from one twin to the next, each taking a turn at slapping his ass silly, screaming giddily.

"Ooh, yeah. Spank that ass. Ooh, yeah. Spank that ass," Chet repeated over and over and over again.

"What the fuck is this?" Ben couldn't help but query.

Chet, suddenly aware that he had an audience, turned his attention to Ben. "Hey, Candyass, care to join us?"

The look of disgust on Ben's face was so thick you would have to use a dirty dishrag to wipe it off. He averted his eyes.

"No. No. No no no no no no no no no no no no no no no no no no no no no no no no no no no no no no no no no no no no no no no no no no no no no no no no! Oh my God, no. Oh my... I... no!"

"What?" Chet innocently inquired.

"Dude, I never want to see that again, ever."

"So that's a no, right? You don't want to join us?"

"Fuuuuuuuccccckkkkkk no!"

"Well, why did you come down here, then?"

"Because you girls were screaming like you were being tortured. And now I can see why."

"Oh," Chet said.

"See you in the morning. I think I gotta take a shit and puke at the same time," he said, and headed up the stairs.

"Last chance, my man," Chet shouted after him. "Come on, the ladies want to see your manly package. Let's see how we compare."

But Ben was long, long gone.

17. The Grits

???

Ooh?

???

Sniff

Aah!

And with that, Brent violently flung himself out of his bed and up the stairs faster than he'd ever moved in his life. The smell of bacon was wafting, and that nerdy little Toucan Sam followed as quickly as his pasty little legs could carry him.

And there it was, shining like a greasy red beacon in the middle of the kitchen table: The largest plate of bacon he had ever seen in his life.

And everyone sitting at the table, staring at him.

Floyd was the only one not staring, for he had his back turned to the hungry mob since he, of all people, was the one at the stove, cooking this crazy breakfast.

"Wow! Holy jeez! Look at all the bacon! And sausage and eggs and toast and grits and bacon, bacon, bacon and I hope everybody isn't as hungry as I am because I'm about to eat it all and why is everyone staring at me?"

"Yo, Brent, you sleep in the nude?" Darnell piped up.

"Franky, that's none of your business, but yeah. Why is this a topic of breakfast conversation?"

And all at once, their collective eyes panned down, and so did Brent's. There it was, dangling like a tiny deflated ferret between his tiny white little legs.

"Oh, shoot!" he said, and bolted back to his room, while everyone burst into laughter at the sight of his little white bottom fleeing down the stairs.

And when he came back up, they were all still laughing.

"Hey, He-Man, hope you're hungry," Buffy giggled.

"Yeah, there's plenty of sausage on the table, if you need some extra," her sister chimed in.

"It looked like somebody took a pin to a tiny little balloon," Chet said. "It was all rubbery and soft. Sort of inhuman," and with that, Chet shut himself up, realizing that maybe he spent a little too much time staring at it. Like if he had to describe it to a sketch artist, he would end up with a perfect drawing of it.

"Baaaa-haaa-haaa," Ben belted out, and the comments continued to fly, and he continued to laugh, until he noticed the look on Brent's reddened face was not one of amusement.

"Hey Floyd, I thought for sure you'd have a problem with cooking, being a man and all," Ben said, abruptly changing the subject. He'd thought of making a clever segue, but he just couldn't think of one. And sometimes an abrupt change in subject is nice.

"Well," Floyd explained, "my momma still cooks the best breakfast in the county, but I think there are two things that men can cook good. One is barbecue- ain't nothin' comin' between a man and his grill. The other is breakfast. 'S long as you stick to meat and eggs and stay away from pancakes and waffles, you're okay. 'Cause I don't know of one man who can Betty Crocker himself up pancakes that are worth a damn."

Kiera's eyes turned downward to the lumpy mushy disaster in the big bowl. "And these are...?"

"Them's grits."

"Ooh, I never had grits before. Aren't they like, coagulated lard or something?" Jonesy threw his TWELVE cents in.

Floyd just stared, dumbly. "Grits are grits, I don't know."

Ben, who considered himself somewhat cultured, decided he'd take a stab at answering. "Grits are a grain, I believe it's hominy?" He looked to Floyd for confirmation, and got only a shrug back. "Anyway, they're boiled and fried and put on the breakfast table for many southern people to enjoy, am I right, Floyd?"

"Ain't nothin' better," he answered.

"I had grits once," Chet said. "At a Waffle House in Orlando, Florida."

"And?" Jonesy said.

"They made me want to punch myself in the face."

"So they were good or...?" Muffy asked.

"I wished I was dead."

"Well, I'll try them," Adam said.

"Me too," said Brent.

"Pass them over."

And before you knew it, everybody, with the exception of Chet, had some grits on their plate, alongside the food that was actually tasty.

Adam braved the first mouthful, and immediately spit it back into his plate. "Oh my God, that's terrible."

"They can't be that bad," Darnell said. The spoon went in his mouth, and the grits flew out, into Adam's plate. "Yo, that grits is wack!"

"This stuff is balls!" Jonesy shouted.

Soon grits were being spat all over the place, ending up back in the plates, on the floor, in others' faces, it was a nightmare.

Curious, Ben finally decided to taste it. It looked a little like oatmeal. Slowly, he raised a small spoonful up to his open mouth. Hmm. He took another small spoonful to his mouth. Hmm. Well, they didn't make him want to punch himself in the face, but... "They're kinda bland."

"Well, that's what the jam and the syrup's fer. You can put whatever you want in it. At breakfast time we put those things in it. When we have 'em for dinner, sometimes we put pork chunks and chili peppers in there. Sorry y'all don't like it."

"That's okay, Floyd. It's an acquired taste," Ben said. "But the rest of the breakfast is fantastic."

"Thanks."

"Hey," Darnell said. "Isn't someone missing?"

"Doris," Kiera said. "I'll go get him."

And as she walked away, Muffy's gaze turned to the porch window, where the girl still sat on the banister.

"Is somebody going to do something about her?" she asked the crew sitting with her.

A burp from Floyd was the closest she got to an answer. How vile! She never in her life had been as disgusted as she was right now, listening to Floyd's belch. She decided to let the subject drop, rather than risk getting an even nastier one.

Kiera returned unaccompanied to the table. "He says he's not hungry. He's just sitting up in bed, playing an acoustic version of Beethoven's Fifth. It's nuts. Hey, is somebody going to remove that chick from the post outside, or are we just going to leave her there all week?"

"No, don't..." Muffy tried to interject, but it was too late. The burp came once again from Floyd's fat, puffy lips.

Which apparently turned Adam's stomach so much that he got up from the table. "Excuse me..." he said, and fled down the stairs.

"And you'll have to excuse me as well," Jonesy said. "But after I get myself a cup of joe I'm going back to my room. This is all too much for me, man."

"I thought you didn't drink coffee," Darnell spoke.

"I don't," Jonesy said with a wink.

18. The Downstairs Bathroom

Adam scurried into his bedroom, opened his bag, and located his smaller bag of toiletries. He scuttled off to the little half bath located next to his room.

He opened up the bag and fished out his toothbrush and Crest Extra Whitening toothpaste. He needed to get the taste of grits out of his mouth, now. That taste, combined with the awful sounds that escaped Floyd's mouth, made him feel like he was going to heave all over the breakfast table.

Brush, brush, brush.

Yeah, brush, brush, brush, but he could still taste it plain as day. It was putrid. He couldn't believe that people ate that bowl of dogshit for breakfast, southern or not.

He had no problem excusing himself from the table. It may have come across to Floyd as just a tad impolite, but he didn't care. He could tell that Floyd didn't like him. Floyd didn't like him because he was different. So if he got a little offended because somebody else didn't like his grits, fine.

The sound of the nail file scraping itself across his tongue sounded like a kitty cat licking a sheet of sandpaper. It didn't feel too good, either, but it seemed to be helping to get that flavor out. Aah, sweet relief. His tongue was actually bleeding after a full minute, so he must have been hacking his taste buds right off. No matter, he was pretty sure they grew back over time.

At last the taste was gone, so he ceased the scraping.

But what the fuck?

That sound... that sound continued. So his tongue wasn't that rough, after all. He knew it shouldn't have been making that noise. So what...?

Still standing at the sink, he risked a look around the room. All pretty peaceful in here. There was nothing that should be making that racket. It must be outside the room. Well, he'd find out what it was soon enough. Just as soon as he washed his face and combed his toupee, he'd...

When he looked in the mirror, he saw where the noise was coming from. The shower curtain was moving. Not much at first, just a faint sway. Could have been the wind. But the more he looked at it, the more it moved, as though it knew now that it had an audience, and soon it was shaking quite violently.

Reluctantly, he turned back to face the curtain, but it was no longer moving. The noise, however- the noise continued. It had gotten louder as the curtain shook more, but even now that it wasn't shaking, the noise continued, even louder than before.

Whatever. He turned back to the mirror to continue washing up, and the curtain was moving again, harder and faster, faster and harder. He turned around again, and it stopped again. Back to the mirror- there. Back to the curtain- gone.

That did it. He needed to see just what was going on. Sure, he was shitting his pants right now, but it wasn't like he had never shat his pants before. I mean, who hasn't, am I right, folks?

He slowly walked toward the curtain. One slow step. Two slow steps. Three slow steps and he was there, with his hand on the blue vinyl drapery. He could neither see nor feel any movement coming from behind the curtain, so it didn't make any sense why the sound was still happening.

Okay, get a hold of yourself, Adam. On the count of four. Ready?

One

oh god oh god oh god

Two

What the hell am I thinking? Oh god.

Three

Run, Adam! Run! Don't open it!

Four

Slide

"Aaaahhhhhhggghhhrhhehvhhghhgthhh!"

His knees gave way under him. Thud. Sitting there, propped up on the shower basin, the top of his head blown clean off, shotgun in his mouth, blood and gray matter rolling down his neck, his torso, to his naked ass, and finally to collect in a bloody pool all around him, was Adam.

But what? This didn't make sense. It looked like a suicide to Adam, but Adam wouldn't commit suicide, and besides that, if Adam was dead, what was Adam doing here looking at him? What?

Uggh. His head was spinning and it was making him quite nauseous. His stomach was going to give way. He crawled his way to the porcelain throne and let this morning's grits plaster the inside of the bowl.

"Blarrffff!" The vomit did not fall quietly from his mouth. It was a tumultuous, dangerous vomit; the kind that comes up and burns the inside of your nasal passage and fills your mouth with a steaming, bloody yark, carrying food that you swear to God you haven't seen in weeks as well as items you swear you haven't seen ever. Food that never quite digests like bits of onion and tomato skin. Food that should have digested nicely, and angered him when he saw that it didn't. He heaved so much he knocked the toupee off his head again. Into the bowl it went.

And as he was fishing it out of the water, there was a knock on the door.

"Adam?" Ben's voice came from beyond. "Adam, are you okay?" And rather that wait for an answer, he opened the door and stepped inside.

"Hey, buddy, are you all right? What made you so sick? It wasn't the gr... Oh my God," Ben said as his eyes fell upon the open shower. "What the fuck is that?"

"You see it, too?" Adam picked his drooly chin up out of the toilet bowl enough to ask.

"See it? Yeah, I see it. We all see it. Adam, what the fuck is going on here? I think I'm gonna be sick."

"Sorry," Adam replied, attempting joviality. "Only room for one, here." His voice was hollow and echoey, like he was talking into a toilet bowl.

"Man, what the fuck is going on here?"

"I don't know." Heeeeaaavvvve!

"What do you mean, you don't know? The curtain is wide open."

"I know, I can't explain it," Adam responded.

"You can't explain what? The shower curtain is open. Obviously you opened it."

"Yeah."

"Don't you realize that's how mildew starts?"

"Huh?"

"You need to leave the curtain closed so it can air out, or before you know it, the shower will be filled with mildew. Haven't you seen those Dateline reports on mold and mildew in the house?"

"I only watch infomercials."

"Well, leave it closed."

Adam picked his head out of the bowl once again, to look at the shower. There was nothing in here. Nothing in here but a loser sitting in front of the toilet with shit in his pants, throwing up for no reason at all, with all his friends standing around watching the spectacle. Nope. Nothing here at all.

"Hey," Ben said, "when you're done vomiting, come on out. We're all going outside to look for little woodland creatures."

"You mean, wild animals?"

"Yeah."

Just saying those words- wild animals- made him sick again. He hated wild animals. He was so scared of them, almost as scared as he was when he found himself dead in the shower. Boy, those were good times. He tried to puke again, but just ended up dry-heaving, so he stopped, took some deep breaths to calm his restless stomach, and flushed.

"Hey," Ben said. "What's that smell? Did you shit yourself?"

"Yeah. Sorry."

"Ah, don't worry about it. I mean, who hasn't shat their pants before, am I right, folks?"

19. The Hike

As the brilliant sun broke free of the thick cloud cover that had promised to swallow the day whole, everyone gathered outside to enjoy the sunshine. There was no telling how long it would last, but night was gone, and chances were it would be coming back sometime today.

Yes, all were present and accounted for, except for Adam, who said he didn't want to go out and enjoy nature, for fear of an animal attack (which wasn't completely a lie, however; he was still shaken up by the shower incident), Doris, who was still in his room, playing Auld Lang Syne, Muffy and Buffy both, who were working on catching up on the sleep they didn't get due to last night's weird sex romp, Kiera, who just felt like lying in bed and staring at the ceiling while she listened to Doris play his six-stringed instrument, Floyd, who still wasn't talking to anybody after they all made such a big deal about how nasty his cooking was, Darnell, who insisted that the black man did not go outside, Ben, who was doing the cleaning he had promised his mother he would do, and Jonesy, who was currently shooting a warm brown liquefied breakfast bean into the inner elbow vein in his left arm. So I guess it was just Chet and Brent.

"Well, guess it's just you and me, kid," Chet said.

"Yeah, I guess, but I think I'm gonna hang indoors, if it's all the same to you."

"If it's all the same to me?" Chet repeated. "No, it's not all the same to me, man. Come on, Brent. You're the only cool one here, as far as I'm concerned."

"I am?"

"Yeah. I mean, I know you're kind of a nerd and everything, but that's cool nowadays."

"It is?"

"Yeah. So come on, don't let me down."

"But what about the wild animals?"

"Do you want to be like Adam? So frightened of his own shadow he's barricading himself indoors for the entire week?"

"But what about the bugs? I'm being eaten alive out here."

"That's what this is for," Chet said, and handed him the can of insect repellent. "So?"

"..."

"Don't let me down."

"All right, fine. Let's go on your stupid hike and get it over with."

"That's the spirit. And who knows? You may even have a good time."

"I doubt that very much."

And off they traveled, dear friends. Over hill and dale they went, traipsing and frolicking. Brent pointed out the various types of coniferous trees along the journey, which he seldom got to see in person. He even realized that he wasn't so frightened of animals after all as they stopped to feed a passing deer.

It suddenly occurred to Brent that he had been leading a very sheltered life. He had been wasting loads of his precious time hanging out in his room playing online fantasy games. He had been using his allergies as an excuse to escape from life. No, this was great. And he reckoned that at this moment, there was no place he would rather be than out here in the wilderness, sharing some precious time with someone who up until recently was just another jock that he had never said two words to in the hallway at school. He didn't even think Chet knew he existed, up until now.

Couch, couch.

"Couch, couch?" Chet asked.

"I meant 'cough, cough,' if you don't mind, your cigarette is making me a little wheezy," Brent said, as he puffed away on his inhaler.

"Oh, hey, no problem, dude," Chet said, as he crushed his freshly-lit cigarette under his heel. "So your asthma's pretty bad, huh?"

"At times it can be downright dreadful."

"Well here," Chet said as he reached into a crumpled cigarette pack and handed Brent a cigarette of his own.

"Are you crazy? That would kill me. If I'm going to die, I can think of much better ways than puffing on the end of a cancer stick."

"Not a cancer stick, dude. This is much easier on the lungs."

Brent got a closer look. "Oooohh, no. No way, man. That stuff's for losers."

"'That stuff's for losers.' Are we in an after-school special? Man, you need to get over yourself. All the cool people are doing it."

"'All the cool people are doing it?' We are in an after-school special."

"I'm kidding, man. If you don't want to smoke, it's all right. But you're missing out."

"On what?"

"On getting stoned."

"Oh, that sounds like a lot to miss out on."

"It's not, really. It's not a big deal at all."

"Then why the guilt trip?"

"Coming out here for a hike when you were scared to death of everything wasn't a big deal, either. Like I say, if you don't want to, that's fine. But don't you ever get the feeling like you're missing out on things? Don't you want to get more out of life? To try more things, to have more experiences? When you're wrinkled and gray, do you want to look back on your life and go, 'Well, I never had a reason to die. But I never had a reason to live, either.' What a waste. Still sitting in your room in sixty years, playing video games. No wife. No kids. No sense of accomplishment. Is that how you want to be? Have you ever even had a beer?"

"Y-y-yes. Sure I have. Lots of times."

"Oh my God, you've never even had a beer."

"So?"

"Hey, whatever," Chet said, as he lit the joint and took a big puff, sucking half the length away. "I rolls 'em small 'cause that's how I rock 'em," he said to himself.

"Fine," Brent said, and held out his hand.

"Attaboy," Chet said. "Now, go easy on it, since this is your first time. Just a small inhale, till you get used to it, or you're going to end up couching your brains out."

"Couching my brains out, just give me the joint," he said as he put it up to his lips and exhaled deeply, as though he was preparing to hit his inhaler.

"What are you doing?" Chet asked, and watched as Brent took an even bigger puff than he did, sucking it down to a roach and dropping it as he burned his fingers.

Then he couched his brains out.

And they continued their journey onward into the forest. Brent didn't see what the big deal was. He was a little lightheaded, sure, but it was most likely from the extreme coughing fit followed by five hits of albuterol.

The chirping of the birds was so loud! But he couldn't blame them. They were just trying to shout over the music.

"Where's that music coming from?" Brent asked. "That's my favorite song. How did they know that?"

"What music?" Chet asked.

And he would have answered, but he was concentrating on the sky. Man, it was so nniiicce. Brent had a hard time walking, because he couldn't take his eyes off it.

"Look at that cloud, man," Brent said, as he stopped short. "It looked just like a jack o-lantern head, but then it just broke apart. Where did it go?"

"Dissipation, dude," Chet explained. "Are you all right?"

"Yeah."

"Hey, buddy. Sorry about that," Chet said.

"About what?" Brent implored for clarification.

"About your big couching fit."

"Cou-hou-hou-ching fit? Woo-haa-haa-haa." Couching fit. That was damn funny. Laugh? Oh boy, did he laugh. And his laughter was infectious, too, because Chet was laughing right alongside him. Okay, maybe Brent was high. If this is what it felt like, it wasn't half bad. Okay, his throat felt like it was stuffed with lamb's wool, and he realized he may have been swallowing involuntarily for the last fifteen minutes, to water it with his own saliva, but other than that, he felt quite nice.

Till the ground gave way under his feet.

"Holy sh... I got you!" Chet said and grabbed hold of Brent's arm.

The force of Brent's fall through the hole pulled Chet down into a prone position on the ground.

"Holy shit, man," Chet said. "What the hell just happened?"

"Never mind that, just pull me up."

Chet looked down into the hole in which Brent dangled.

"Man, it sure is a long way down. I mean, we are on a mountain and everything, but I didn't realize we were so close to the edge of the cliff. You must have just stepped in a weak spot. This sucks. I'm getting all dirty and whatnot. I think you jarred my shoulder. Still, I'd much rather be up here than down there."

"I jarred your shoulder? You grabbed me!" Brent screamed.

"Yeah, well, I didn't have to," Chet argued.

"Whatever, just pull me up!"

"What's the magic word?"

"Please! Please pull me up!"

"No, that's not it."

"What is it, then? I'll say whatever! Come on!"

Brent watched as the look in Chet's eyes turned menacing. This was not fun anymore, not that it ever was to begin with. He knew that Chet was no longer joking.

A silence swept the two boys. Brent was hushed because his lungs were running out of breathable air. It seemed as though Chet was deep in thought; deep within himself.

Nothing but the chirping birds and crickets.

At last, Chet spoke.

"You know, man. There are a lot of things that bug me. Every damn one of you fucks bug me. None of you know who I am. Not one of you, do you understand?"

Sweat was starting to form on palms- there was no telling from whom.

"Do you understand me?"

Brent nodded. He could not speak. His lungs were growing weaker, and so was Chet's grip.

"Everybody thinks I'm a dumb jock. That I have no feelings. Well, I'll tell you what. I have feelings, just like the rest of you! I hurt too, dad! Do you hear me? Do you?"

Brent nodded again. Oh, please please please.

Sweatier and sweatier. Slowly slipping.

"Just because you suck your coach's dick in the locker room does not make you gay. I only did it once! Okay, twice! But that's it! I'm a man, dammit! A man who just occasionally happens to be attracted to other men, that's all. That doesn't make me..."

He was interrupted by a squeak from Brent's lips.

"And you. Do you know what really bugs me about you, dude?"

He shook his head no.

"You say humidity bothers your lungs. Your asthma acts up when it gets too humid outside. But you sleep with a humidifier. You say that helps you breathe. Does that make any sense? Where's the logic in that?"

Brent just dangled.

"Speaking of humidity, your hand is awfully sweaty. I'm losing you. Hang on," he said, and reached his other hand around Brent's arm and pulled him up.

He immediately reached in his pocket for his inhaler and took a couple quick puffs as Chet brushed himself off. A tear escaped his eye.

"Oh, hey man, I didn't mean to scare you. I was just playing. Here, you're all dirty," he said, and brushed the leaves from the little guy's hair.

"Why are you crying? I wasn't going to let you go. What do you weigh? FORTY pounds soaking wet? I could have held you there all day. Now come on, let's get back to camp."

And with that, they turned around and headed back.

"Oh, and one more thing, dude," he said as he put his arm around his shoulder. "If you ever tell anybody about this I'll fucking kill you."

20. The Bonfire

The legend around these parts
In the northern Vermont woods
There lives a man
With digits missing on his left hand

'Three-Fingered Willy', they call him
For they know not his God-given name
Some say he's just a lonely old man
Some say he's a monster

His face is so hideous
That he hides it in a paper sack
And all you can see, if you look hard enough
Are two dead eyes peering through the holes

He wanders the streets alone
Carrying only a sickle
In his hand with two fingers gone
In his other hand, his long-lost wife's head

He murders tiny women
Then their tiny children

Harm's Way

And when he's done, he puts away
The man of the household

It was not long ago
That old lady Henderson went out shopping
Her man waited long at home
But the wait was all in vain

It was not long after that
The baby disappeared
With nothing left in her crib
But two bloodstains on her sheets

The man did not wait around
To get his punishment
He went out in the barn, with a .45
And died by his own hand

The chickens and pigs devoured him
Leaving nary a trace
When Willy came in to collect his reward
He thought the man had fled

Now, old Willy roams the night
Wandering among the camps
Searching for any sign
Of where the man could be

Yes, he walks through the darkness
Approaching each bonfire
One by one, until...
Oh, my God, behind you!!!!"

"L-a-a-a-me," Muffy said to Ben. "Buffy's got a better one. Show 'em."

And she sure did show 'em. She grabbed her shirt and pulled it up over her head, exposing her braless chest. She balled the shirt up, and into the bonfire it went.

"Ooo-kay?" Ben said. "I don't see what the point in that was. Not exactly scary, but nice."

"Thanks," Buffy said, without blushing.

All were present and accounted for, save Doris, who was in his room merrily playing Stairway to Heaven for the umpteenth time, and Adam, who had calmed down a little since this morning, but was seriously afraid of, as he put it, "the gruesome creatures of the night".

Suddenly, Jonesy jumped off of the log he was sitting on, cracking his head on a tree branch overhead, but not really paying much attention to it. "So I suppose somebody wants me to say something. Huh? Do you want me to say something? Floyd?"

"I...don't..."

"Ben?"

"Say what?"

"Kathy? Mary?"

"Who?"

"David Koldsveldt?"

Darnell: "Jonesy, what the suck are you talking about?"

"Fine, I'll just come out and say it. GooooodddddDAMMIT!" he said, and quickly had a seat.

Darnell: "I just can't believe I'm out here toasting marshmallows. Old white pillow of sugar, darken yo' skin. 'Tis a black man's burden at times to join in."

All: "Shut Up, Darnell!"

"Fuck, I can't siddowwnnn!" Jonesy said, and whacked his head yet again, a really good one this time, enough to make him bleed a decent amount.

"Dude," Ben said, "are you still all jacked up on the coffee from this morning?"

"Must be must be yeah that must be it."

"I didn't think you drank coffee," Buffy said, as she slung her naked titties about.

"I don't," he answered. "And I didn't."

"Then what..."

Kiera spoke up, never once taking her eyes from the dirt canal she was digging with her marshmallow-roasting stick. "He injected it."

"Way to go, dude," were the only four words Chet had said or would say all evening. He was still thinking about what he'd done. He was trying hard to recall exactly what it was he had said to Brent on their little walk. Did he say too much?

"Thanks thanks a lot. You should try it sometime. Beats the hell out of drinking it. Sure does."

A good thirty seconds of silence followed, and then: "Whoop-dee-fucking doo!" he shouted again, as he danced around the campfire, knocking over Darnell's beer in the process.

"Woah, there man," Darnell blurted.

"I'll get it," Floyd said, and reached the beer before Darnell even had a chance to bend down.

He brushed off the rim and handed it over. "There you go, Darnig."

"Tha- huh?"

"Well, I'm going to bed," Floyd said before he had to explain what he just called Darnell.

"Yeah, me too," Kiera said. "Before I feel the urge to stick this hot marshmallow stick in my fucking eye."

And with that, one by one, they all turned in.

21. The Night Talk

Adam, are you awake?" Brent wondered aloud, as he turned on his humidifier. "Man, you missed a swell bonfire. I just got to see boobies for the first time. Boobies! Buffy just took her shirt off for no reason whatsoever and tossed it into the fire. Can you believe it? I mean, I know she's the ugly twin, but still, they're pretty nice. Not that I have anything to compare them to.

"And I think you almost missed a good fight. There's getting to be a lot of tension between Darnell and Floyd. I have a feeling Floyd's a racist. I think I heard him call him a nigger. Man, if I was Darnell I would have punched his lights out. I felt like doing it right then, even not being Darnell, but who am I kidding, really?

"And maybe I'm crazy, but I think Jonesy may have a drug problem. Today he shot up coffee. Right into his vein. I know heroin's not good for you, but as long as you don't overdose, you're not going to kill yourself, but coffee? Who knows what that'll do to you? But boy howdy, was he hyper.

"Oh, earlier today, boy I'll never forget that. I went on a hike with Chet. He convinced me to go even though I didn't want to. He got me to smoke pot for the first time. Boy, today was a day of firsts. Let me tell you, it wasn't as bad as I thought it was. I take back everything I ever said about pot smokers. It felt good. No wonder people do it. I don't know if I could do it all the time, but I would certainly do it again.

"And then... Oh, I'm not supposed to tell anybody this. I have a feeling I can trust you, though. So here goes: I almost fell off the edge of the mountain today. I went through a sink hole and right in the nick of time, Chet grabs my arm. He saved my life, and I am grateful, but he held me there for the longest time. I swear to God he was going to let me go. He started freaking out. I don't even think he knew who I was. He called me dad, and talked about how he has feelings, and about how he has oral sex with guys. I don't know. Don't tell anybody this, okay? But then he pulled me up and said he was just playing around. But something tells me he wasn't. I don't feel safe around him.

"Well anyway, good night Adam. See you in the morn."

22. The Revelation

All were gathered at the breakfast table once again. Floyd had decided that he was going to have another go at cooking the most important meal of the day, despite the critique he received the previous morning. Sans grits, this time.

Yes, sans grits. Unfortunately, however, Darnell thought he would be helpful and cook up some cream of wheat, thereby eliminating any possibility of Floyd thinking everybody should just give his grits one more chance.

And cream of wheat was fine, for Darnell, but nobody else liked cream of wheat. It was slightly better than the grits, but only slightly. Ben tried pretending it was oatmeal as he was eating it, but that didn't work. That never works.

Ben was trying really hard to force down his third mouthful of the shit when he noticed Brent standing at the top of the basement stairs. Foamy drool rolling down his chin, a yellow river of thick snot coming from his left nostril only, eyes rolled way back in his head like he was in a trance of some sort. Knees shaking like he was doing the Watusi, whatever that was.

Now, this was a funny look for him, and Ben would have thought he was joking, were he somebody else. However, Brent was not the type who had much of a sense of humor. Perhaps this would change slightly, now that he had apparently discovered weed, but now was not the time to be thinking about what would or would not happen to Brent's sense of humor in the near future. All that mattered was at this point in time, he was not joking.

"What is it, Brent?" Ben said. "What's wrong, buddy?" Did Timmy fall down the mineshaft?

Brent just stood there and continued to drool and shake, but now he slowly lifted a shaky right arm to point down the steps, without saying a word.

Quickly, they all got up and raced each other down the stairs and into Brent's room.

"What the actual fuck?" Chet blurted.

"Adam?" Ben asked, and slowly approached the bed, alone, to where Adam lay.

Obviously dead, his jaw locked open, wider than any human could ever stretch it; his eyes also open wide. It appeared that rigor mortis had set in and was still in effect.

"Adam?" Darnell dumbly said, as they all approached the bed, one by one, as slowly as Ben had.

And there he still lay, oblivious to all the goings on around him, mostly because he was dead, his arms thrown up and locked there, as though something had really surprised the hell out of him enough to end his life. The tendons in his neck all showing through his skin as though he was frozen in a silent scream. And there, upon his head, also dead, lay a festering, fly-ridden beaver. The great natural dam-building northern woodland creature, perched there, heedless of what was happening in the room, mostly because he, too, was dead.

"I don't get it," Muffy said. "What just happened here?"

"Don't you understand?" Brent answered from the doorway, suddenly out of his stupor, which caused all to turn their heads. "Somebody switched Adam's usual toupee with a dead animal. That's what killed him. He went into shock and died. He's dead. He's fucking dead!"

Ben, so stunned that he heard Brent swear for the first time in his life, could barely get out a further explanation. But he did anyway. "Adam was scared to death of beaver."

"You could say that again," Chet snickered.

"Ha-ha," Ben said sarcastically. "Not just beaver, you imbeciles, but all wild animals."

"Yes, but this beaver was obviously dead when it was swapped with his toupee," Buffy continued the argument. "Why would he be scared of a dead beaver?"

"I don't know," Ben said. "But it doesn't matter why at this point. All that matters is how. Obviously there's a rabble rouser and a malcontent in our midst."

And boy, was he sorry he said that. Immediately the eyes of the crowd once more settled on him.

"Oh no," Ben said. "No no. Not me. Why is everybody looking at me again?"

"This is retarded," Kiera said, and stormed back into her room, slamming the door on herself and Doris, which they could hear from all the way down here.

"Listen, Ben," said Buffy. "If you look at the dynamics of the entire situation, you're really the only obvious choice. It's your cabin. It was your idea to drag us all here, even though the majority of us did not want to go. There was a fucking dead girl on the porch when we arrived. You're the only one who knew where the cabin was. Plus, this obviously happened last night, during the bonfire. You went inside to get snacks, and if you don't mind me saying so, you were in here for way too long to grab a couple of bags of chips and some beer."

"Now hold on just one goddamned minute. I was not the only one to come in here last night." He looked at Chet. "You came in here to get more beer. And you," he pointed to Darnell, "went in to take a shit, if I remember correctly. And you too, Floyd. And as I recall, you didn't like Adam very much. And what about you, Brent? You spent the night in the room, for god's sake. In fact, I think we all went in at one point last night, so don't be so quick to point the finger at me."

"You're right," Buffy said. "Never mind."

"And as far as I can tell, that dead girl on the post had nothing at all to do with Adam. Unless..."

"Unless what, Ben?"

"Yes, please tell us."

"Do tell."

"No, the thought is too difficult to bear," he said.

"Oh, come on, already."

"Fine. Unless that girl had everything to do with Adam. Unless whoever did this is not one of us. Unless somebody else is here with us."

"What do you mean?"

"Do I have to spell it out for you? The killer is here with us, but is not one of us. The killer is someone else. Like the murders that happened in the other camps? Maybe he's back."

"Murders at the other camps?" Buffy asked.

So Ben explained it now, to all of them. It didn't make sense to keep secrets any longer

This time Darnell spoke. "I know, man. Adam told me the whole thing, right after you told him. And I thought to myself that it was a bullshit story if I ever heard one. I could tell the moment you started spewing that shit that it was all a big lie to scare him."

"To scare him?" Ben replied. "To scare him? You think I wanted to scare him? I was trying to explain the girl on the fucking banister. That's what I was doing. That girl was enough to scare the shit out of all of us. And you think I wanted to scare him more? What the fuck? How dare you. How dare any of you. I figured I owe you an explanation, but you know what? Fuck you. You don't deserve an explanation. And when we all start dropping like flies here, you'll see."

"Man, that was no explanation. The dead girl on the banister was just that- a dead girl on the banister. There's no killer on the loose."

"Well, there is now," Brent replied.

Which shut them all up.

"Does anybody want to say a few words?" Ben asked, as they stood staring at Adam's dead body, which now lay in a pile with the anonymous dead girl ten meters or so into the woods.

There were no takers.

"Brent?" Ben prompted.

"Yeah, okay," he said, and stood up proud beside the corpse.

He cleared his throat. "I'm not really all that good at things like this," he said, "so I guess I'm just going to read a passage from the Star, if you don't mind," he said, and pulled a copy of it out of his back pocket.

"This was his favorite article, from a few years ago," he explained. "This is his favorite passage. 'When asked for comment, Mr. Willis said, "I wish them all the happiness and success in the world. All I have ever wanted in life was to see Ashton happy."'"

A weak round of applause followed.

"And one more, if you don't mind." He cleared his throat one more time. "'When asked for comment on the recent marriage of Tom and Xenu, Ms. Alley said, "I wish them all the happiness and success in the world. All I ever wanted in life was to see the two of them happy. And to keep off the weight. Because damn, do I look good. Thanks, Jenny."'"

"Thanks, Jenny," they all replied.

Tears were welling up in Ben's eyes.

"What's wrong, Ben?" Muffy asked.

"What's wrong? Other than this?" he said, as he gestured to the carcass. "I guess I'm just really upset because Adam and I were so close. Man, he was like my brother. He and I would tell each other anything. And there's nobody else I can say that about. Not any of you, or any of my family, or anyone else. My god, I was the only one he..." He stopped dead in those tracks.

"The only one he what?" Kiera, who had rejoined the assembly, asked.

And when Ben didn't answer, she did for him. "The only one he came out to?"

Ben, stunned, nodded.

"Yeah, I was the only one he came out to, too," she confessed.

"Me, too," Jonesy piped in.

"Me, too." Chet.

"Me, too." Muffy.

"Me, too." Buffy.

"Me, too." Darnell.

"Me, as well." Brent.

"And me." Floyd.

"Floyd, you too?" Ben asked, incredulously.

"Nice usage of unnecessary adverb," Brent said.

"Thanks," I replied.

"Yeah, that little quarr told me, too. And I hated him fer it. God hates fags. And this little homo siyunnned against God. And ratt now he's roasting in hell fer it. But I can keep a secret, I don't care who you are, so..."

"Wow," said Ben. "I need a minute to reevaluate my friendship skills," he said, and so concluded the ceremony.

23. The Two-Holed Privy

Buffy walked up to the privacy shed, which was inconveniently located way too far from the camp, and rapped lightly on the door.

Tap-tap-tap. "Martha?" That was her little pet name for her sister. Mainly because it was her real name.

Buffy's real name was Bertha, which may or may not be relevant later on in the story.

No response.

Tap-tap-tap. "Martha???"

And from inside, a very weak: "Go away."

"Come on, are you going to stay in there all day?"

"I said, go away."

She slowly opened the door to find Muffy, fully clothed, sitting on top of the wooden box with a hole in it.

And rather than scold her sister, Muffy asked, "How did you know where to find me?"

To which Buffy responded, "How do I always know where to find you? Wherever there's an outhouse around, you'll be in it eventually."

The privacy shed, or privy, was probably built in 1792, and probably hadn't been cleaned out since then. Actually, I don't know if outhouses actually get cleaned out, or if the holes just get filled in and the shed gets moved, or what the procedure is, but I really have no interest in finding out. You probably know better than I, so go with what you got. There had been no need for the outhouse here, not since all the camps now had indoor plumbing, so the toilet shouldn't have stunk this bad, but it did.

Buffy took a seat on the wooden box next to her sister. This was, in fact, a two-holer. So there was no real privacy in the privacy shed. I guess back in the days in which the outhouse was built, nobody gave a shit. As Buffy swatted some flies from Muffy's brow, she noticed a profound sense of sadness in her eyes.

"What's the matter?"

"What's the matter?" Muffy repeated. "Have you not been paying attention to all that has been going on around here? This little trip to the woods is turning into one big nightmare."

"Well, it has been a little unusual, but..."

"Unusual? Unusual? Putting chili powder in your milk, that's unusual. Susan Boyle covering Pantera songs, that would be unusual. This, this is way beyond unusual at this point."

"All right, fine. You win. This is one big nightmare, as you call it. But we came here to have fun, didn't we?"

Reluctantly, her sister nodded.

"So come on. We've got the rest of the week to enjoy ourselves. Let's not let a few snags in the plans ruin the rest of our trip."

"You're right... I guess."

"Now let's get out of here. It really stinks in here."

"I know."

"Like, worse than shit."

"Yeah."

They had walked down the privy trail toward the camp when they saw Chet.

Chop.

Chop.

Chop.

He was chopping wood for the nightly bonfire, hence the

Chop.

Chop.

Chop.

He stopped in mid-stroke as he noticed the twins walking by.

"Ladies," he said. "Hey, I just thought of a funny book-author combo. Just the Tip by Haywood Jablowmi. Huh-huh. Pretty funny, huh?"

"It would be," Buffy answered, "Were Jablowmi a real last name. Like Horny and Single by Anita Mandalay. That's funny."

Chet's jovial expression turned sour, and he ignored the girls, favoring instead staring at the large axe he was wielding.

"You know what I like about an axe, ladies? I like the fact that no matter how dull it gets you can still chop through things. Like a really dull knife won't cut well. A really dull razor won't cut well. They both have to be really sharp to do their job. But a dull axe will cut almost as well as a sharp one. Because it's all in the power. The long handle, you see. That's what gives you the power. A hatchet doesn't have that. An axe is much better. But I like to keep my axe sharp. As sharp as a block of New York cheddar. Yessir. 'Cause I respect the weapon. Do you respect the weapon?"

But at this point he was talking to nobody, for the girls had already continued their leisurely pace onward toward the camp, and were a good twenty yards away.

"Hey ladies!" Chet shouted. "You forgot your gift!"

And with that, he threw the axe as hard as he could, sending it spinning through the air. Spinning, spinning, spinning, and landing at the ground about ten feet shy of Buffy's leg. She briefly turned around to acknowledge the axe, and then they both continued their leisurely pace toward the camp.

"You know," she said. "There's something about that guy. I can't put my finger on it, but doesn't he seem a little odd to you?"

"Odd?" Muffy said. "In what way?"

"I don't know. Maybe it's nothing."

"Do you think he's gay?" Muffy asked.

"Maybe that's it."

"'Cause he really didn't seem into the other night."

"Yeah."

"Usually guys are all about the twin action. He seemed like he was just going through the motions."

"Yeah. And I'm pretty sure that one time he called me 'coach'."

They walked into the house and into the kitchen, to see Floyd fixing a rather large hoagie, fit for three people, at least.

"Hey, Floyd, how about you leave some ham for the rest of us?" Buffy said.

Floyd gave a sarcastic smile. "Still plinny of cold cuts t' go around. And don't ever talk to a mayunn like that. Don't you know your manners?"

"Blow me."

"Hey, that's remindin' me of a joke."

"Don't care."

Muffy chimed in. "How can you eat at a time like this?"

"Same as I always do," Floyd answered. "With my teeth."

"What teeth?" she asked.

"The TWENTY-SEVEN I have left. I'm only missing one."

"Which is a requirement where you're from, right? At least one tooth has to be missing."

"Why, if you weren't a lady I swear I'd..."

"You'd what?" Muffy said. "You're hardly what I'd call a southern gentleman. So say what you have to say."

"No, never mind. Anyway, I'm eating 'cause I'm hungry."

"Floyd's right, you know," Buffy said. "We have to eat. Pass the mustard, fatty."

24. The Questions

They had all gathered around the bonfire once again, for yet another night of pure camping fun. This time nobody wanted to be indoors alone. After what happened the previous night, nobody wanted to take any chances.

Nobody, that was, except for Doris. Ben could just barely hear the lovely strain of the "Too Fat Polka" coming from his magical six-stringed love interest.

"You know, I've been thinking," Ben started, which got some groans from his fellow campers. "I know Doris is a weird guy in general. I'm sure Muffy and Buffy would agree." He looked over at them and got slight nods from both, but also looks of apprehension- they weren't sure they liked where this was headed.

"But don't you think it's really weird that the guy never wants to leave his room? I mean, I've never even seen him leave to get a bite to eat or anything. The moment we arrived here he went straight to his room and he hasn't come out since. I know he really likes his guitar, and that's cool. Aside from Hendrix, and maybe even including Hendrix, I've never heard someone master that thing the way he has. But someone who'll play a Frank Yankovic classic on guitar? A little too weird, if you ask me."

"So where are you going with this one, Ben?" Buffy spoke up.

"Just weird, is all I'm saying. And I don't think it's too far of a stretch to think that maybe he's the kind of guy that just may go off his rocker completely."

"Don't see what you're getting at," Buffy prodded, although she knew damn well.

"I'm just saying. Aside from Adam, out of all of us, he was the only one indoors the whole night last night."

"Are you saying you think he may have killed Adam? 'Cause I hope that's not what you're saying," Buffy said.

"No, I'm not saying I think he may have killed Adam," Ben said. "All I am saying is that he was the only one of us that was indoors the whole night last night. And he is the only one of us that totally fell under the radar. His name didn't even come up once when we were hurling accusations."

"You were the only one that was hurling accusations, Ben." Now it was Kiera that spoke up. "And from what I remember, your name was the only one we brought up."

"Yes, but even still, Doris was the only one I didn't mention, then. My bad. I'm just saying, that out of all of us, he's the only one that hasn't had a word to say. He just stays locked in his room, as though he has something to hide."

Kiera continued. "Jesus Christ, Ben. I was completely willing to forget about last night, as were all of us, but now you're bringing it up again. Didn't you say that "the killer" was on the loose again? I was willing to buy that. You had me convinced. Subject dropped. But now you're bringing it up again. You feel the need to overconvince us. But all you're doing is digging a hole. Further and further. And let me tell you something about Doris. He's a kind, sweet, gentle guy who wouldn't swat a mosquito if it was biting him. I'd believe I was the killer before I believed that he was."

"Are you fucking him?" Chet asked.

"Would you shut the fuck up for once?" Kiera demanded. "And even though it's none of your business anyway, I'm not fucking him. I just feel a connection with him because nobody understands him. I know what that's like. Nobody understands me, either."

"Oh, I know. Nobody understands you at all, Kiera," Chet said. "Oh, I'm going to paint my nails black and dye my hair black and put on lots of black eyeliner and wear nothing but black and think dark thoughts and listen to dark music and pretend that nobody understands me. That'll be cool. You can't go on doing that forever, sweetie. Do you see any forty-year-old goth kids? No, because sooner or later they either shut the fuck up and kill themselves already or they grow up."

"Dude, she's going to blow," Floyd said.

"No, that's just it. She's not going to blow. Because she couldn't possibly allow herself to expend that much energy. It would require her to break out of character."

"Fuck you, Chet. And fuck you and you and you and you and you and you and you. Fuck all of you," she said.

"And with that, she storms off. Typical."

"Jeez, man. You didn't have to be so hard on her," Brent said, to which he got a look in return that made him cower in fear, bringing back all that happened yesterday.

"Did you hear that, folks?" Chet said, the look of anger burning so deep in his eyes they were setting small fires in Brent's soul. "The boy said 'hard on'."

"Anyhoo, who's up for some s'mores?" Ben asked.

"Yeah, pass that bag of marshmallows on over here," Darnell said.

"Oh, did you change your mind about the white man's snack?" Ben asked.

"Well, you know, I've been thinking about what this snack represents. Look-a-look-a-look-a-look-a-look-a here. I'm taking the white marsh-mallow. I'm impaling it with my spear. Now, I'm holding it in the fire until it blackens. You see, that's when it becomes more than just a boring white pile of mushy junk. When you blacken it, it becomes special. Then, I put it on the brown graham cracker with some even browner chocolate. That's when it becomes spectacular."

"You're really overdoing it, Darnell," Ben said.

"What do you mean, brother?" he asked.

"He means you're being too much of a nigger," Floyd said.

"And there it goes," Darnell said, not looking surprised at all. "The N-bomb. Listen here you fat fucking cracker. You fucking piece of shit. You may talk like that around all of your redneck friends, but that shit doesn't fly here," Darnell said.

"I meant that he was trying to be something he's not," Ben clarified. "Which maybe you could stand to do more of. I'm surprised Darnell's not kicking your ass right now."

"MLK, baby, MLK."

"But you need to cut that shit, or you'll be walking home. I'm not going to listen to it anymore. And nobody else wants to, either," Ben said.

Floyd got up, and headed in. "It's a fine day when a man can't even speak his mahnd anymore. Have a good night." He stopped in his tracks. "Oh, and Darnell. Being a colored person- is that better?. Being a colored person in Vermont, are you less lackly to get hit by a snow-mobile in a storm?"

To which he received no response from anyone.

"What? That was a legitimate question."

"Goodnight, Floyd," Ben said. And then, as an afterthought, "Hey Floyd?"

"Hmm?"

"So what's up? You don't like blacks, you don't like gays, you don't like Mexicans. You know what I think?"

Floyd sighed. "Whut?"

"I think you're just prejudiced against anyone who isn't...well...you." And with that, Floyd went into the house.

"You know what I don't get about black people," Brent started.

"Here we go," Darnell said.

"No, I'm just curious. There are a lot of black people down south, where people like Floyd live."

"Yeah?"

"And here in Vermont, where Floyd lives but doesn't belong, people are a lot more accepting of everyone. It doesn't matter what color skin you have. I think it's that way everywhere north of the Mason-Dixon line."

"Yeah?"

"But there's a severe lack of black people here."

"Yeah."

"Why is that?"

"I don't know."

"Well, I know that's where their homes are, and there's no reason that people should have to run from bigotry, because that's just letting them win, but it's been this way for hundreds and hundreds of years. And if you look at evolution, species, over time, tend to migrate to where they feel the most comfortable and to where they're accepted into the community. But it doesn't happen with people."

"Yeah."

"I just think it's weird, that's all."

"I guess."

"Well, folks. I've about had it for the night," Jonesy said. "So if you'll excuse me..." and he left.

Now, every party has that one guy. The party will be kind of at its wind-down phase, but people will still be there, sticking around. But then there's that one guy or girl, that once they leave, it's the cue for everyone to start leaving, one by one. The thing is, it's not always the same person. And it's kind of arbitrary as to who it is. There's no explaining it. The party just has to be at that point. Although not everyone has that power. Jonesy never had that power. Typically, he'd be the one at the party that was so fucked up that he'd never know when the proper time was to leave. Well tonight, by golly, he had that power, because one by one, everyone went inside, and that was it for the night. Good for you, Jonesy. Bravo.

25. The Quiet Night

It was a cold November evening and I should have worn a coat. I shivered, waiting for the ferry boat to carry me to you."

It was beautiful, a masterpiece. Of course, everything that Doris played was beautiful, a masterpiece. Kiera never realized he had such an angelic singing voice- the kind of voice that you could just melt into. And she didn't think anybody else in the world listened to the Tear Garden. They were perhaps the most beautiful musical happenstance ever. The only thing in the world that made her feel both amazing and melancholy beyond belief. A band that was a side project, one of those forgotten bands that lived in some unknown corner of the universe, and here Doris was, singing one of their best songs. He knew her too well.

He was radiant. Through the power of his guitar and his voice, he was able to make her feel a little less dark. It had been forever since she'd had any light shining on her, and she rediscovered how amazing that felt. He was stirring up things in her she never realized were lying around waiting to be stirred up. She was getting wetter by the second. And by the dull lamp of the second floor bedroom she surrendered her body.

Jonesy stirred the beer for a good ten minutes, contemplating its pissy yellow color. He was not a drinker, by any means. Drinking led to alcoholism, which was the lowest of the low, in his book. In this day and age, when everyone was fully aware of the dangers of alcohol, it was still funny or maybe pitiable to be an alcoholic. People either loved drinkers or they felt sorry for them. He felt neither. But whatever, everyone had their vices, especially him, so he wasn't one to talk.

No, he wasn't a drinker, but desperate times called for desperate pleasures, and he was really running out of options at this point.

There. He'd stirred it enough, he thought. There was no sign of any more bubbles rising to the surface- it was officially flat, which is exactly what he wanted. He had no idea what carbon dioxide would do if injected into your bloodstream, but he was sure it wasn't good. He slammed the needle down into the glass, pulled up the plunger, and got ready for the ride.

"Adam, are you awake? Man, you missed a swell bonfire!" He shouted to the bare walls.

What was he doing? He had the feeling he was cracking up. He was losing it, and he didn't like it one bit. All his life he'd always been in control of his own little universe. A small universe it was, sure, but it was all his. Now it felt like it was just crumbling away like some old statue.

He was just now getting it. The finality of it all. His roommate was dead. Dead. He'd never had that happen before. Nobody he knew had ever died, as far as he could remember. And although he wouldn't consider Adam his best friend or anything, he had felt some sort of bond with him. They were both outcasts. Neither one of them had many friends. They had a really good talk the first night there, and Brent really liked him. And now, no more.

The tears rolled freely down his face as he turned the humidifier on, and he thought, I probably don't need this tonight. It will be humid enough with all my tears.

26. The Burn Victim

Eleven A.M.

11:00 A.M. and most were up and about.

The only issue with that was that they didn't go to bed all that late, and *all* should be up and about. All except for Doris, that was. But even he was making his presence known by playing a beautiful rendition of "Cat Scratch Fever", making it sound way better than the original. And good for him, because Ted Nugent is a giant douche bag.

Jonesy had been up and was now in his room, possibly trying to figure out how to inject a syringe full of maple syrup into his body. Kiera was sitting outside on the porch, watching the birds fly to and fro, appearing as though she thought it was all just lovely. Floyd had his fat ass parked on the living room sofa, watching TV, pissing and moaning that they didn't get shit for channels out here. Darnell was outside doing something, trying to put himself as far away from Floyd as possible, before he finally decided to go crazy and beat his head in with a lead pipe. Muffy and Buffy were in the bathroom getting ready; he could hear them giggling. Chet was outside chopping more wood (!!! The woodpile was getting ridiculous. They had enough there to keep them warm through the next ice age). Avid Cunningham was happily brushing his one tooth, thankful they didn't take that, too. But you probably don't know who Avid Cunningham is, so I won't bore you with the details of his life. Ben was sitting alone at the kitchen table, taking inventory of where everyone was and what they were doing at 11:00 A.M.

All except for Brent. Brent was not up and about. Brent was nowhere to be found. Brent was usually an early riser. There was no way he was still in bed. No way.

Don't tell me, Ben thought to himself as he ran quickly down the stairs toward Brent's room.

He heard a faint low humming coming from the other side of the threshold. He knocked softly on the door. "Brent?"

He pounded hard on the door. "Brent, are you in there?"

He opened the door, not waiting any longer for a response. He knew what he would find, and I'll be goddamned if he didn't find it. But nothing, none of his experiences as a cop, none of his time spent in 'Nam, could prepare him for the sight he was greeted with when he poked his head in the room.

"Oh, for fuck's sake already." Brent was indeed still in bed, or what was left of him. He only knew it was Brent because everyone else was accounted for.

His partially skeletal remains were sitting up in bed, half-propped against the wall. He was hunched over, just as he was a lot of the time when he was having a coughing fit. It appeared that this coffin fit was more severe than any other one he'd seen him have, as part of his throat was dangling from his mouth- one of the few bits of flesh left. His eyes were absent.

He had no more skin, and the pieces of flesh that still clung to his bones made him appear as though he were dry-rubbed in a secret blend of spices and had been slow-cooking for hours.

"Brent?" he said. "Brent, are you okay?"

He went over to him and tried to shake him, to wake him up. The bloody bits of flesh stuck to the sheets and just sloughed off the bone, like a nice tender rack of ribs.

What the hell happened in here? This macabre scene could not have been done by human hands. What could have melted the flesh from Brent's bones so thoroughly?

The humidifier was humming and rattling away; it had run dry and was frankly not too happy about it. The noise was maddening.

He reached over onto Brent's nightstand and shut it off, and noticed when he did that there was not much left of the inside of that machine. The clear plastic water tank was all scratched and scarred, and appeared to be almost melted in spots, and the water intake valve and such were destroyed. Its internal organs looked like...

Well, like Brent.

It was suddenly clear to Ben that whatever killed Brent also killed this machine.

But why? If you wanted to kill Brent, fine, but why bother taking the time to destroy this machine? It didn't make sense.

That's when it hit him. Something ate away at the humidifier. There had to have been something other than water in there. Whoever killed Brent knew damn well that he used his humidifier every night and filled it with...

What? What did they fill it with? Some sort of acid? Would acid do that? Could acid vaporize in a humidifier and send out fumes toxic enough to make someone hack their throat out and melt out their eyes and then eat away at their flesh before they had a chance to get away?

And who the hell cared, anyway? Brent was dead. Dead. That's all that mattered. And now he had the task of telling the gang. Hey kids, another dead one. Isn't this a fun trip? Aren't you glad you came?

Phooey.

27. The Birthday Girl

Okay fine, it was a muffin. But recently she came to the realization that the only thing that really separated muffins from cupcakes were a few misplaced grains of sugar. It was all a big scam.

Yes, it was a muffin. A lemon poppy muffin, to be exact, which was her favorite, with peanut butter in lieu of frosting and a lit match in the middle to serve as a candle.

It was Buffy's idea. It was her sister's birthday, and there was no way in hell she was going to miss out. She loved this day too much. In past years they had always made such a big fuss about Muffy's birthday that Buffy kind of got left out. But that was okay. Muffy was the pretty one, so she got all the attention anyway. She was used to it. Though their parents loved them both very much, it was plain to see that their mother favored Muffy. They both knew what it was like to get by on looks alone. They had a kinship. Buffy got by on her intelligence, and though it seemed she was encouraged in her academic endeavors, she knew deep down that her mother resented her just a little for being so bright. She could see the chip on her mother's shoulder, and usually she was okay with it, but sometimes it made her so mad that she just wanted to kill everyone. She wanted to put her hands around all of their little necks and just squeeze and twist until they were no longer breathing.

But hey, water under the bridge. Plus, they weren't technically born on the same day, anyway. They were born FIFTEEN minutes apart, close to midnight, so Buffy's birthday was actually tomorrow. And she didn't really care enough about her own birthday to really make a big stink anyway.

Plus, this would help take Muffy's mind off all of this death stuff, which really seemed to be getting her down.

She joined in the chorus as they sang happy birthday to her sister.

"Lemon poppy, my favorite," she said.

"Hurry, blow out the match. It's about to fizzle," said Doris, who actually came out to help celebrate his cousin's birthday.

She closed her eyes, and made a wish. She wished that the rest of them would survive the week, but the match had gone out long before she blew, since it took her so long to articulate that thought. Everyone knew what she wished for. Everyone saw she didn't make it. Nobody said anything. Just a superstition.

Right?

28. The Dick

Muffy stopped mid-chew on her makeshift birthday cake when she saw the '98 black Crown Victoria pull confidently into the driveway.

"The hell?" Ben said as the door opened, and he watched a man dressed in a smart gray suit and a gray soft wool fedora with a fine silk band around the brim plant one leg firmly on the gravel, followed by the other, shut the car door with some sort of odd authority, and make a bee line straight to the porch.

He stopped for a minute to ponder the newel post, which was still covered in blood stains and crusted vaginal juices. He took one well-manicured fingernail, scraped a few flakes off the wood, and held his finger to his nose.

He wore a deep, contemplative smirk, the kind you may see Bogart wear in an old movie. In fact, he sort of resembled Bogart, in a weird way.

Changing his mind about going straight to the door, he decided instead he would take a look around the grounds, walking nonchalantly to and fro. It didn't take him long to discover the three bodies tossed in the heap in the woods. He took a pad out of his jacket pocket, scribbling a few notes as he examined the mess.

Apparently satisfied, he turned back and made his way once again to the front door.

Knock knock knock.

Ben opened the door. "Yes, can I help you?"

"Ted Jenkins, Private Eye," the man explained, and showed documentation that confirmed it. "May I come in?"

Ben was speechless. A private eye? What the hell was a private eye doing here? Was he investigating the murders? A private eye? Don't they only handle cheating spouses nowadays?

Tired of waiting to be invited in, he pushed Ben aside and stepped in.

"Out of my way, son. I have work to do."

The nerve!

"Hey, you can't just come barging in here like that!" Ben said, appalled.

Jenkins got two inches or so from Ben's face. "Maybe you didn't hear me. I said 'Ted Jenkins, Private Eye'. Now, that gives me a license to go where I want, when I want, how I want, until I get answers. You hear me, son?"

"Uh, yes?"

"You're darn right, you do. Now, I'm gonna take a look around here, and I suggest you don't interfere with my job. I don't interfere with yours."

"I don't have a job."

Jenkins quickly turned on his heels so he was once again facing Ben. "Maybe that's your problem. Maybe you need to get one. Maybe then you'll have some responsibility. Instead of coming up here, partying, getting all footloose, tossing your cares to the wind. Now, if you don't mind..."

Ben let him go. He watched him as he went into the kitchen, opened the fridge, and helped himself to a Diet Coke. He watched him go up to the second floor. He heard him walking into each bedroom. He watched him go downstairs, taking extra time in Adam and Brent's room. He heard the mad scritch-scritch-scratching of the pencil making contact with the little pad. He did not follow him. Maybe he had a point. Maybe he should just let the man do his job. Maybe he wold come up with some answers as to just what had been happening around here.

The detective came back upstairs. "I need everyone front and center in the living room. I have a lot of questions, and I need answers," he demanded.

He barged into Doris' room. "Get out here, music man. You're part of this, too."

Doris didn't move.

"Into the living room with the rest of them," he said.

Doris still didn't move.

"Now you listen here, son. I used to eat little boys like you for breakfast. Why, it used to be all I had to do was nod my head at the county judge and they'd lock you up without a second thought. Nowadays everyone has rights. Well let me tell you right now, chorus boy, the world today stinks. It's better you and I face that fact right now. Now, I have a few questions to ask everyone, and the last time I checked, you're part of everyone. So scram. Out in the living room."

Doris didn't budge.

"You heard me, scram."

Finally, Doris decided at the second scram to get up, albeit leisurely, and head out into the living room.

The detective got to the top of the landing and was greeted with the sight of Floyd sipping the Diet Coke he had placed on the kitchen table so that both hands could be free to write in his little pad.

"Hey, what's the big idea? That was my diet cola, you hear me? Mine. And you have to be kidding if you think that for one second I believe that you actually drink that stuff, fatso. Now, somebody get me another Coke and everybody else have a seat. Let's get this show on the road."

"What's this all about?" Ben asked, as he handed the detective another soda.

"I'll ask the questions around here, pal. What's this all about? I'll tell you what it's all about. Its about murders. That's right. Murders. Plural. More than one. As far as I can tell, there are three dead here. Coincidence, or is somebody going on a killing spree? That's what I'm here to find out."

"But..." Ben began.

"Don't but me, pal. The last one who butted me got charged with obstruction of justice, for standing in the way of an investigation. Wanna spend the rest of your life in jail?"

Ben shook his head.

"Then speak when spoken to."

"Ha-ha. He got you, there, Ben," Chet said.

"You, funny boy. Where were you Friday night?"

"I was in bed. We all went to bed early."

"Where were you Saturday night?"

"At the bonfire."

"Where were you Sunday night?"

"Bonfire."

"Hmm. You sure like bonfires. Coincidence?"

"Coincidence how?"

"Bon-fire. French term, meaning good...fire. Never really cared much for the French, so I don't use their language. Parlez-vous American?"

"Uh, yeah."

"Because around here, that's what I speak. Voulez-vous jailtime?"

"No."

"Because that's where you're headed, if you don't straighten up and answer my questions."

"I have been."

"I'll get back to you. And I'll use the term 'campfire', thank you very much. No French connotations there."

"Actually, I think the word 'camp' actually did derive from the French," Buffy spurted.

"You two are double trouble, I'll tell you right now. Trouble with a capital 'T'," he said, indicating the twins.

"Two beautiful broads, both twins. Boy, I'll tell ya. In my day, just looking at them was enough to get you some serious jail time. Nowadays, two young teenage girls can walk around looking both innocent and sexy at the same time, turn everybody into a pedophile."

"Boy, everybody must have been in jail in your time," Jonesy ejaculated.

"Listen here, buddy boy. I'm no stranger to the junk. It's been around for a long time. I've seen mothers put it in their baby's milk to help them sleep. Turn them into addicts. I've seen butterballs as big as this kid," he pointed to Floyd, "turn into walking sticks. Sticky walking zombies on two legs. So don't tell me I don't know your world, son. I've lived in it."

"I never said you don't."

Doris, who knew he was the only one not at the bonfire, was nervously drumming on the table. Kiera was singing along to the beat.

"I bought a ticket to the world. But now I've come back again."

"Would you please stop that infernal racket. What was that awful tune?" he asked Kiera.

"Spandau Ballet."

"Span what? Gibberish. Probably rock and roll music. Full of nothing but gibberish. Rock and roll is what went wrong with this country. Turned old men to dust and old ladies' hearts sour. Rock and roll killed America," he said, and asked Kiera, "And what's with you, sweetheart? Dressed in black. Wearing black makeup. Your soul black, too? Why, there was a time when the men liked their ladies to wear lipstick as red as a new Ferrari, and the ladies loved to wear it for them, beautiful skirts with fishnets and garters and cute little hats. Nowadays all a girl wants to do is look as unappealing as possible."

"But you just told them the opposite," Darnell said, gesturing at the twins.

"And you, sir. Was a time when people like you played piano in fine restaurants and bars. Made quite a living doing that, and got the respect your people deserved. Nowadays all you like to do is walk around carrying firearms. How about it, son? You carrying?"

"Uh, no."

"Uh, no. Speak up, son. Be proud. Stand on your own two feet. And for the love of God, stop hanging around with these yahoos," he said.

Then, Jenkins continued. "Listen, the facts are this. One girl, dead. Massive wounds to her female parts. One boy, dead, skin and flesh melted clear off his body. Another boy, dead, no apparent injuries. And one dead beaver. All lying in a pile in the woods on your property," he said to Ben. "Seems to me someone had a vendetta against these innocent kids. Don't know who, but I'll figure it out. Just give me time," he said, and got up to leave.

He turned once more to the crowd. "And don't think you kids can continue to cause trouble. This is a quiet town and I'd like to keep it that way," and stormed out the door.

Darnell watched out the window as he got in his car. "What...the...fuck...?"

"Your guess is as good as mine, man," Ben said. "Your guess is as good as mine."

Floyd looked around- looked at Chet, looked at Jonesy, looked at Ben. "L-L-L-LUNCHHHHH!"

29. The Lunch

The long slab of bread lay supine on the cold laminate countertop, its two sides open spread-eagle, anticipating the addition of other ingredients.

But first, the thick white milky glop, the mayonnaise, clinging to the knife like a thick spent load, dreading the inevitable drop toward the sub roll, but ultimately giving in, deciding that in reality this was what it was born to do. The knife coming up behind it and spreading it thin only on one side of the roll. The bright yellow mustard soon followed, shooting out of the plastic bottle like spunk from a rigid staff, ready to infiltrate the bread with its seed.

The cold, crisp, dark green romaine lettuce sat there on the counter, waiting its turn. Surely it would turn this sandwich into something extravagant, something fit for a royal family. But alas, only one leaf was pulled from the bunch. A heart-leaf it was, but split lengthwise down the middle, and laid end to end on the bread, it was just a useless object, resembling nothing of its former self.

The tomato, red, ripe and ready, was anticipating the serrated blade to hack it to pieces. And when the moment came, it felt so damn good. The blade sliced. And sliced. And sliced. Until it was in a thousand paper-thin slices. So thin you could read official court documents through them. And soon they too were placed carefully on the bread.

The meat came afterward. Ham, salami, roast beef, mortadella, capicola, the list was endless. Followed by cheeses both American and Swiss.

The sandwich, just barely hinged together in the first place, finally gave when it was forced shut, bursting with tasty goodness.

Darnell watched it all, from the edge of the kitchen. He watched as Floyd made that gigantic sandwich and he thought, Enough! Enough already with this bullshit.

He walked over to Floyd. "Hey."

"Hey," Floyd said back.

"I hear you make the best subs in town."

Floyd shrugged. "I do okay."

"Cool," Darnell said. He couldn't take it anymore. The tension had to stop.

"Listen," Darnell began. "I know in the real world we would never be friends. You'd probably be trying to beat the shit out of me or I'd be blowing your head in with my MAC-9."

"Ten," Floyd corrected.

"Huh?"

"MAC-10."

"Right. Well, either way. I know once we get home we'll probably go our separate ways, but do you think for now we could just put all the bullshit aside? Sweep it under the rug?"

"You mean, 'Cain't we all just get along?'"

"Something like that," Darnell said, staring at the floor, embarrassed to swallow his pride.

"You know somethin'?" Floyd said. "You are the first black person to ever approach me like that. The first one. I mean, where I come from, there are some places where blacks and whites git along fine, and there are some places where they don't. I'm from one of those places. But maybe it's time to change. New place, new outlook, you know? I don't know, maybe I been wrong all along about colored people. Maybe I been wrong about lots of things."

"Yeah, maybe. And maybe I've been wrong about southern people."

"No, not really. There's a lot of ignorant southern folks. A lot of assholes. But there's a lot of good ones, too. Maybe it's time for me to become one of the good ones."

"That's great, man. Good for you."

"Here," Floyd said, and cut his sandwich in half. "I could stand to cut down on my portions anyway."

Darnell took a bite of the sandwich. "Holy shit, man. You should open up your own shop. This is damn good."

"You think so?"

"Yeah."

"Well, it's just a sandwich. Wait till tomorrow. I'm gonna make some gumbo."

"Really? I've never had gumbo. I've always wanted to try it though. Haaayyyy, wait a minute. I thought you said you didn't know how to cook. I thought you said you could only do breakfast."

"Well, I'll let you in on a little secret. Fact is, most southern men know how to cook. It's in their blood. They just don't want to admit it. Dinner time's a time for men to gather 'round and drink beer and shoot the shit, while the women work in the kitchen. If the men were in the kitchen, it would take away from their shit shootin' time."

"Wow. Hey man, I'm learning a lot about you. Thanks."

And Chet, being a dink as usual, called from the living room: "Why don't you guys make out or something?"

To which Darnell replied, "You'd like that, wouldn't you?"

"N-n-no," Chet said, and let the subject drop. It was best he didn't say anymore.

It was best for everyone.

30. The Freak-Out

Television is an interesting tool. Forget education. Forget entertainment. Forget boredom relief. It is nothing more than a pacifier. It's a machine that can effectively and without fail completely extinguish the minds of the masses in a matter of minutes. We have a nation full of drooling, blabbering idiots with their asses parked in front of flashing boxes, at once absorbing everything and nothing. A total brainwashing device if ever there was one. Hitler would have been proud.

Tonight the group decided to place themselves in front of the box, since Ben was lucky enough to have a few channels of cable out here in the middle of nowhere. Kind of makes you wonder why on earth someone would want to pay a cable bill for a cabin they haven't been using much as of late, but as you can tell by now, very little makes sense here.

Some show was on. A reality show where teams of people had to eat dead chickens for prizes. Gross.

This was soon followed by a talk show where parents had to confront their own demons, and realize that all the blame for their family being so fucked up rested solely on them, not their kids. Weird.

This was followed by yet another reality show where some people were doing something, and they got some sort of thing if they could do whatever it was they were doing in the fastest time, or the slowest time, or something.

And in the midst of the three hours of television they had all been watching, a cavalcade of commercials. Exactly seventy-three minutes worth of nothing but stuff people were trying to sell you. Like Gatorade.

"Man, I can't believe I forgot to buy some fucking GATORADE!!!" said Ben, and threw the remote across the room, busting the battery compartment off it, sending the twelve AAA batteries it took to run the thing scattering across the living room and kitchen floors. "I LOVE THAT STUFF!!!"

"Jesus Christ, Ben. Calm down. Gatorade is a delicious beverage for the thirst demon in all of us, but there is no reason to become hostile," said Chet, and then added unnecessarily: "Besides, if we had some, you wouldn't get any anyway. Simon would probably inject it all."

Jonesy's face turned FORTY-TWO shades of red. "What?!?"

"Are you saying you wouldn't?"

"First of all, fucker, don't ever call me Simon. Second, don't act like you know me. You don't know anything about me. You don't know what it's like for me. My body is screaming out for something I don't have. So I have to make do with what there is. And third, coming from a fucking drunk, I really take that to heart."

"Drunk? What the hell are you talking about?"

"Drunk. How many beers have you had tonight?"

"None of your goddamned business."

"And nobody but a drunk would say that."

Now it was Chet who was turning red.

"Oh yeah?"

"Good one, Chet. I guaran-fucking-tee you that aside from cigarettes, alcohol has killed more people than any other drug. And will continue to do so forever, because it's acceptable. Oh, you're all so high and mighty. Jonesy's a junkie. But you all drink to some degree." He looked at Chet again. "And don't tell me you don't smoke weed. Even through the beer breath I can smell it on you."

"I have glaucoma."

"Uh-huh. And don't tell me you've never taken pain killers before."

"Okay."

"Recreationally."

"Fine."

"But I guess in pill form, opiates are fine. And what about your cake, Muffy?"

"Don't drag me into this."

"What kind of cake was it?"

"It was a muffin."

"What kind of muffin?"

"Lemon poppy. Okay, I get it."

"So chewing it is fine, too. But somehow, using a needle is crossing the line into obscenity. Fuck you guys. Fuck all of you. I'm going to bed."

Fine. He was going to bed. It was 11:00 anyway, and there was nothing on but the news, and who the hell wants to watch that?

31. The Apology

So," Ben asked Chet as his face appeared in the doorway, axe in hand, "are we done tearing each other apart?"

"What do you mean?" Chet asked, not knowing what Ben meant.

"We're all tearing each other apart," Ben clarified.

"I still don't get it," Chet said, still not getting it.

"Nothing, it's just... I brought us all here to have a good time. That's all I wanted was for us to have some fun, and for all of my friends to get to know each other a little bit more. And all we've done ever since we've gotten here is fight. It doesn't make sense."

"Doesn't make sense? Come on, Ben, I thought you were smarter than that. Dude, none of us were ever really friends to begin with. None of us really talked to each other in school. We're all from different cliques. We have absolutely nothing in common, except for you. None of us really like each other all that much. So forgive me for saying so, but to throw us all together in a cabin for a week was kind of a stupid idea."

"Yeah, I guess it was, wasn't it?"

"Oh, and on top of that, people are getting fucking murdered around here. Tends to make people a little edgy, usually."

"Yeah, I understand," Ben said.

"Do you really?" Chet replied. "Because it seems to me that you're the only one around here that's remaining perfectly calm. No conflicts with you, are there, buddy?"

"Exactly what are you saying?" Ben asked, not knowing exactly what Chet was saying. "Because if you want to have some tension with me, you can, you know. I'm not beyond getting pissed off."

"No, no," Chet conceded. "But Jonesy deserved it, man. There's no place in the world for a junkie.

"Don't be ignorant, captain. You're not perfect, either."

"I'm not?"

"Come on, man. You think I don't know?"

"Don't know what?"

"I know all about you, dude."

"The fuck is that supposed to mean?"

"Who's your best friend in the whole world?" Ben asked.

"Well, you," Chet answered.

"And a lot of other people would say that, too, not to sound conceited or anything. And do you know why I'm such a good friend to all of you? Because I'm genuine. Because I give a fuck. So I know things about all of you that nobody else knows. Like you. I know something about you that you would never admit to anyone. Something you would probably never even admit to yourself."

Chet didn't ask what. He knew; he just didn't want to hear it spoken aloud.

"You've all got stuff, man. Everybody's got stuff. I've got stuff, too. You know some things about me nobody knows. That's what makes a good friend. So don't pretend that you know Jonesy's story. You have no idea what makes him do what he does. And I'm not going to go into it, either. All I will say is, none of us are perfect. None of us have an ideal home life."

Chet was staring at the worn carpet under his feet, moving strands of fabric this way and that to create poop patterns in the weave. He looked up at Ben. "You're right, man. I'm a giant ass. I'll go talk to him."

"Good idea," Ben said, "I think he's in the bathroom. Come to think of it, he's been in there a while." And as he watched Chet walk away, he thought: I am a little gassy, but I will not fart here, for fear that it may be more than gas.

And in the distance, Ben heard it. First, it was a "Hey buddy, you got a minute?" And then it was a primal scream the likes of which Ben had never heard before.

"Aw, what the fuck?" Ben asked out loud, but he already knew the answer.

"Shit, man! I'm sorry! I'm sorry!"

Chet repeated it, over and over and over again. I'm sorry. I'm sorry. I'm sorry.

When Ben stepped into the room, Chet stopped, and turned to him. "I did it, man. I killed Jonesy."

And Jonesy was in fact dead, the needle still in his arm, his body upright on the toilet, empty fast food containers strewn about at his feet. Thank you verah much.

"Oh, man," Ben said.

"I killed him, man. I drove him to this."

All the commotion drew a slow crowd, until everybody that was left alive, with the exception of the guitar player, was standing in the doorway, déjà vu, déjà vu.

Ben didn't really feel like consoling Chet. Right now he just felt like getting the fucking body out of his house before he had a nervous fucking breakdown. But this moment called for his best friend skills. And like some Super Power, they came on their own.

"Listen to me, man," he said, grabbing Chet's sobbing head and turning it toward his own. "You didn't kill him. It wasn't you. Jonesy lived with ridicule his whole life, and you think one argument with you drove him to this? Get over yourself."

"Then why? Why is he dead?"

"It happens with heroin addiction. If you don't get help for it, eventually you OD. It was inevitable."

Buffy spoke. "I don't think it was heroin that killed him."

"What?" Ben asked. "Look at him. I mean, obviously it was..."

"Remember? He was injecting all this weird shit because there was no heroin left." Buffy asked.

"She's right, man," Darnell said.

"He was out," Kiera said, through tears.

"Then what?" Ben asked, and pulled the needle out of Jonesy's arm, making a sick sucking noise.

There was still some substance left in the needle. He held it up to the light over the vanity and examined it. They were all right. It wasn't heroin. It was a cloudy orange liquid.

He took the top off the syringe and a faint familiar odor slowly wafted from the vial. It was not at all unpleasant. He took a bigger sniff.

"Smells kind of like Florida," he said.

"Florida?" the crowd asked.

"Yeah." He put his finger up to the vial and tipped it upside down, to get a little on it. He put his finger up to his mouth.

"Don't do it!" the onlookers screamed.

"Don't worry," he said. "I have a hunch..." and tasted it. Now he knew what the smell was. The taste was undeniable. He took vitamins every morning. And he took a lot of these when he was sick. It was a bitter, acidic taste, citric, as though they actually made the vitamins from oranges and grapefruits.

"This here, friends, is Vitamin C."

"Vitamin C?" they asked.

"Yeah."

"You mean to tell me that after all the shit he's injected over the past couple of days, what killed him was Vitamin C?" Chet asked.

"Yeah."

"But how did he liquefy it?" said Muffy. "And why would he shoot it?"

"Can't you see?" Ben said. "Don't you guys get what's going on here? He didn't inject Vitamin C. Somebody left it for him. He was probably thinking it was something else. Something he'd just cooked up. He never liked Vitamin C. It gave him a bad allergic reaction whenever he tried it."

"So somebody pulled the old switcheroo?" Chet asked.

"Seems to be a trend here, don't you think?" Ben asked. "First, somebody switches Adam's toupee with a beaver. Next they switch the water in Brent's humidifier with acid. Now this. What we're dealing with here, people, is a swapper."

"A swapper," Muffy repeated, slowly, feeling the word on her tongue.

"It's like somebody's bad idea of a practical joke," Ben said. "Only it's not practical. And I'm not laughing."

32. The Stew

Floyd?"

"Yeah?"

"Is that smell what I think it is?"

"Depends on what you think it is."

"Is that gumbo?"

"Heh heh. Yeah, it's gumbo."

Ben smacked his lips in anticipation. "Uh, where did you learn to make gumbo?"

"I was born knowin' how to make gumbo."

"But aren't you from Georgia?"

"Yeah."

"I didn't know there were any Cajun people in Georgia."

"Oh yeah. See, a hundred years ago or so, there was a big hubbub in N'orlans. See, all of a sudden, German immigrants was comin' into the area. Now Germans, being naïve and all, didn't know nothin' bout Loosiana. And suddenly, as quickly as they came in, they was droppin' like flies, on account of the swamp gators. Now, the cajun people, they already knew about the gator problem, but to them it wan't a problem. See, gators never bother frogs. But, soon as they got a taste of human blood, they started eatin' the French, too. Lot of 'em got scared, drove some of 'em clear out the bayou."

"You're full of shit," Ben said.

"Yeah," Muffy agreed.

"And I thought the boys down south couldn't cook anything but breakfast."

Floyd gave Ben a stern look. "Shhh." He'd already explained himself to Darnell, and feared he said too much. The secret of the boys down south shouldn't be let out.

"Well, it smells great."

"Thanks. That's my secret ingredient."

"And what's the secret ingredient?"

"Ginger."

"Ginger, well that's very masculine."

"Hey, now. See, it's the spice of the ginger that brings out the heat of the peppers."

Their culinary class was cut short by Chet barging in. "Can you get AIDS from fucking a dead whore?" he wanted to know. And since nobody could answer that (I mean, although totally inappropriate, it was a legitimate question), they didn't bother pondering it for too long.

"Well, I see you're feeling better," Ben remarked.

"Yeah well, I figure we're all gonna die here, so why bother spending the rest of my days all gloomy?"

"That's uplifting," Ben said.

"Floyd?" Chet asked.

"Yeah?"

"Is that smell what I think it is?"

"Depends on what you think it is."

"Is that dwarf pudding?"

"Heh-heh. Yeah, it's gumbo."

"Great, I love jackoff stew. Mind if I take a peek?"

"Be my guest."

Chet opened the lid, and the smell dealt him an uppercut to his chin. POW! Such an incredible aroma, he just had to ask, "Can I have a taste?"

"Well, it won't be ready for a couple hours yet, but I guess 'twouldn't hurt."

Chet grabbed the giant wooden spoon that had formed a nice puddle of gumbo juice on the counter and dug right in. He held the spoon up to his lips. "Holy shit this is good did you put ginger in this?" he asked with much enthusiasm.

"Yeah."

"Wow," he said, and dipped the spoon back into the pot. Only this time he didn't come away with a mouthful of stew. This time he came away with a mouthful of awe. "Wh-huh?" He asked. "Dude, what's the stringy shit?"

"Stringy shit?"

"Yeah," Chet said, and tried to get a spoonful. Try as he might, however, he was not successful. "Are you trying to choke us to death or something?"

Floyd looked into the pot, and there was indeed stringy stuff. "You got any tongs, Ben?"

"Left drawer, all the way down."

Floyd grabbed a pair of heavy duty barbecue grill tongs from the drawer and went back to the pot. He latched onto the stringy material and pulled up. Startled, he dropped the head on the floor, and the partially boiled skin fell from the face as it hit.

Floyd looked as though he was going to faint. He gave a nice Cajun, "Hoo-lawd!"

Chet looked disgusted. "Oh, come on with this bullshit. This is getting old quick." He let out a bellow the likes of which no one had ever heard before, grabbed the steaming hot head by the hair, and ran off with it into the woods.

"Was that Adam?" Muffy asked.

"Yup," Buffy answered.

"Where the hell's he going with that?" she asked.

"Beats the hell out of me," she answered.

33. The Art of Welding/ The Epiphany

They decided as a unit to leave Chet alone; just let him do what he needed to do with the head. I mean, Adam was dead. He was mostly eaten by maggots and wild animals by now; there was no bringing him back. So if running around with his severed head proved therapeutic for Chet, then let him be.

But they reached a point, after listening to the hooting and hollering and whooping and yelling insanities, inanities and profanities, that they just couldn't take it anymore.

"Who wants to go see what he's doing?" Ben asked.

"I will," Jonesy answered.

Oh, my bad. Jonesy is no longer with us. I guess I should start keeping track of this shit.

"I will," Darnell answered.

"Really?" Ben asked.

"Naw, I'm just playin'. You white peoples is crazy!"

"Fine, for fuck's sake, I'll go. Why do I have to do everything around here?"

"It's your fucking cabin!" Kiera snapped back. "It's your fucking cabin; this was your fucking idea; and you can go fuck yourself!" And with that, she stormed off to her room. Toward the sweet sound of "The Chicken Dance".

"You know, you sure do a lot of storming off!" Ben yelled after her.

"Bit-gummit! What the flap? Doesn't make sense to meeeeee!!! Why can't they just R.I.P.? Huh? The head and the flies! The maggots and the lies! Ha!"

Ben approached the madman slowly, surreptitiously, so as to not disturb him too much. Chet seemed to have become a bit of a loose cannon since the murders started happening, and there was little sense in rattling his cage any more than it already was.

He was a good fifty feet or so away, but already he could smell the strong, unmistakable odor of burning flesh. Not since Vietnam had he remembered smelling anything so ghastly.

What the fuck was he doing?

"And with this, I shall make one out of many. Several out of the few. Dominis mo'biskits."

A blue flame shot out of Chet's hand. Or so Ben thought at first, until he got up closer and saw that this blue flame was shooting out of a yellow cylinder he was holding. MAPP gas. He was torching Adam's head!

"Uh, Chet?" he said, as quietly as he could while still allowing himself to be heard.

Chet, startled, whipped around, the flame almost setting Ben's clothes on fire. "Yes what is it."

"Well...uh...what...are you doing?"

"I am trying to make Adam whole again. He did not deserve to be in two pieces. Nobody deserves to be in two pieces!" he answered, using his most logical tone.

"Are...you...trying...to weld...his head...back onto his body?" he asked.

"Why...yes...Captain...Kirk...I am!" he answered.

"That's not going to work," Ben said.

"Why?" Chet demanded to know. "I demand to know!"

"Well, for one, you can't just weld with a can of gas. You also need a cylinder of O2."

"Where can I pick one of those up?"

"Your local hardware store. You also need a welding rig and everything else. But that's not even the point. You can't weld human flesh back together. Or any flesh, for that matter."

"Why not?"

"Well, welding only works on metal. All you're doing is cooking the flesh." He pointed to spots on Adam's neck. "See here, and here? Scorched. A better option would be to get some solder and try to do it that way, but I still don't think it will work."

"So what am I going to do?" Chet asked.

"Well, shut the torch off, for one."

Chet turned the knob so the flame shrunk, and finally disappeared.

"And listen to me carefully, dude. Look at me. Listen. Just let it be. Put the torch down on the ground and walk away. Adam's dead, man. All these guys are dead. There's no bringing them back."

"Don't you think I know that?" Chet asked.

"Frankly, Chet, I don't know what you're thinking right now."

"The murders and everything, that's bad enough. But whoever's doing this, they need to for fuck sake let these people rest with some fucking dignity!" He said, and threw the torch on the ground and stormed off toward the camp.

"Why is everyone storming off?" Ben asked himself. "Hey, wait up!"

He caught up to Chet, who was busy muttering to himself.

When he saw Ben at his side, he decided to talk to him instead. "You know, man, I've been thinking."

"Yeah?"

"Yeah. You ever get a craving? Like you want something to eat? You want it so bad you can taste it, almost, but for the life of you, you just can't figure out what it is?"

"Yeah, that happens to me sometimes. It doesn't happen so much anymore, just once in a while."

"Happened a lot more when you were younger, right?"

"Yuh."

"I think I figured out what it is."

"What is it?"

"Evolution."

"Evolution?"

"Yep. Remember how we were talking about evolution the other night, about how evolution affects migration, and how black people should all be up north by now?"

"Sure do."

"Well, that got me thinking, if that's the case, then why haven't squirrels been naturally selected enough so that by now it's instilled in them a fear of crossing the road in front of oncoming traffic?"

"Good point," Ben said.

"Thought so, but then I thought that cars have only been around for a hundred years or so. A very small window in the history of the squirrel. Given time, I think they will learn to avoid the road."

"Okay."

"Then I started to get hungry. I got that craving I was talking about. And it dawned on me. Evolution!"

"Evolution."

"Yes! Evolution! You know how they say that deep down in the human brain, there is still the reptilian part, from way back when we were reptiles?"

"Yes."

"Well, they showed that our brains have evolved, but deep down, we still have the raw instincts that reptiles have. Those thought processes are instilled in us."

"Right."

"And our brains and our taste buds and everything have evolved with the knowledge of what is good and safe to eat. As a species, we crave these foods."

"Right."

"But over time, species die out. Animals that we have once eaten have perished. Plants and fruits that we may have dined on have fizzled and left the planet."

"Okay."

"But the deepest parts of our brains, the parts with all the history, still crave those foods."

"Wow."

"And as we get older, we get those craving less because we teach our brains that we're never going to get those foods we crave, so we just suppress that urge."

"Christ."

"Whatcha think of that?"

"I think you should have been a scientist. You just hit upon something brilliant. I never knew you could be so inquisitive. But what does this have to do with the murders?"

"The murders? The murders? Fuck, man. Is that all you want to talk about? Why'd you have to bring that up? I'm just trying to get my mind off it. Can't you just leave well enough alone?"

Chet continued his storming, all the way into his room.

34. The Escape Artist

plea to the world outside
i tap tap on the window, whispering quietly:
hello? hello? can anybody hear me?
my whispers become shouts become screams
but there is dead silence from the world outside

the yellowed rotten teeth of sadness
sink themselves into my neck
spreading their leprositic disease
but nobody sees it happen from the world outside

everytime i touch myself i burn my own skin
the fire inside me is smoldering, simmering
the endless torture of existence is but a game to me now
trying to keep it up for the sake of the world outside

my heart my brain my blood my bones
my breasts my legs my steaming cunt
make me girl, human, alive
but somehow keep me separate from the world outside

and maybe someday they'll win
maybe someday i'll be one of them

and this poem will be a mystery. who wrote this?
some depraved creature, not someone from here
can't be
not from this world outside

but till then i'll smile and laugh
and join in their games and fun
but knowing that there's a chance, there's a good chance
that I will never ever ever be part of the world outside

She closed the journal, not knowing if the poem was technically "finished" or not, but it didn't matter. She put the pen down and gave a deep sigh. She went to her suitcase and pulled out the buck knife her daddy had given her when she was THREE. She didn't quite know if she was going to do it or not, especially since Doris was watching. But she was left with very little option. And when she thought about it, they all were. She'd been feeling like this for a few years now, and she couldn't see any light beyond the darkness. There'd been suicide attempts before, but her mother, who was a spitting image of Doris Day playing June Cleaver doing a really good Martha Stewart impression, minus the cold-hearted bitchiness that Ms. Stewart is capable of, thought it was cute. She always thought it was a cry for attention, and it seemed to her that she could make her daughter feel better with ice cream and shopping trips. And she liked the ice cream and shopping trips, don't get me wrong. But they never did much to cure the darkness that was eating her soul.

All that aside, she knew that she really had no choice but to take her own life. She was going to die anyway; they all were.

Doris broke in the middle of the second bar of "Sweetest Taboo". He put the guitar down for once, and performed the rare act of speaking. "Kiera?" he dared ask.

"What?" she asked back, clearly distraught.

"I don't think that's really a good idea."

"What business is it of yours?" she snapped. "Listen Doris, I like you. You are perhaps the coolest guy I know. So don't take this the wrong way, but please butt out. You don't know me, not really. Fuck, I don't even know me all that well. So if you don't want to watch, turn your head or go in the other room or something. But I have to do this. I have to," she said, as the knife blade sunk a little deeper into her forearm. Not drawing blood yet, but it would soon.

"All right, fine," Doris said. "Go ahead and do what you gotta do. I'll go watch TV or something," he said, and walked out of the room, slamming the door.

The stares of wonderment fell upon Doris as he came down the stairs and into the living room. This was only the second time he'd left his room all week, so they knew there had to be an important reason.

"I need your help, guys," he said, clearly exasperated. "Kiera's trying to kill herself."

"What?" said Darnell.

"You don't say," said Floyd.

"Buggary!" shouted Ben, and raced upstairs, threw open the bedroom door, and rushed in to find Kiera, knife in right hand, drawing it across her left wrist, sending the tiniest stream of blood trickling down to her elbow and dripping on the bed, leaving little round stains all around where she sat.

And as she pushed the knife into her arm a second time in an attempt to draw an even deeper river of blood, Ben rushed the bed, tackling her and nearly knocking both Kiera and the headboard into the next room.

But the knife still stayed wedged in her arm. Try as he might, that little black-haired bitch was strong. Any attempts he made to pry the knife away from her were futile; she was holding on for dear life.

"Help!" he shouted as Darnell, Floyd and Chet both rushed into the room. Did I just say "both"?

"Leave me alone!" she shouted. "Let me die!" But as strong as Kiera's will was, it was no match against the strength of four almost-men prying her arm away.

Chet pulled the knife's tip out of her arm and flung it into the hallway.

"The fuck is wrong with you?" he asked.

"What the fuck is wrong with you guys?!?!?!?!?!?!?!?!?!?!?!?!!?!?!?!?!?!?!?!?!?!?!?!?!?!?!?!?!" she asked not-so-calmly, as you could probably gather.

"What's the matter, Kiera?" Ben asked, in a much nicer way. "What's with all the wanting to take your own life stuff?"

"We're all gonna die!"

"Well, yeah, but..." Ben began.

"Yeah, but?" she repeated. "Yeah, but?!? Are you for real? There should be no but. I should go: 'We're all gonna die!' and then you should go: 'Yeah,' and be done with it. Yeah, but? No way. We're all going to die. There's no getting around it. Some of us may die horribly. I mean, look at what happened to Brent, for fuck's sake! His flesh fizzled away! Just fizzled! And Jonesy injecting that shit!"

"It was only vitamin C," Chet began.

"Doesn't matter. That shit ate him from the inside out. Couldn't have been comfortable. And Adam with the beaver! Jesus! And that girl, on the post. Torture! And you expect me to wait around and die? Possibly be painfully tortured? I don't think so! I'm taking it in my own hands! I'm going peacefully, and if you guys want to stick around and be mutilated, be my guest."

"But can't you see, Kiera?" Ben asked. "You're letting the killer win. Don't kill yourself. It wants to drive us apart. It wants us to die. And you're doing it. You're letting it win. Don't let it win, Kiera. Don't let it win."

"Ping," said Kiera, as though this answered everything, and after that, the discussion of suicide never came up again.

35. The Card Game

Ben opened the fresh pack of playing cards, knowing damn well he was in for a lengthy shuffle. The playing cards were all in order by suit, from 2 to A, as they all were when you first purchased them. He didn't believe these playing cards were from a casino, as they didn't have any edge clipped or holes through them, but they did say "Circus Circus" on each card, like placards posted to red diamond wallpaper.

The stiffness of the cards made them almost impossible to shuffle, but it made them quite easy to deal, as he was doing now- six to himself, six to Darnell.

"You know, Darnell, the very fact that you know how to play cribbage should disqualify you from being black," Ben joked.

"Fuck you, honky. And we forgot to cut for crib."

They did. Darnell drew a 3, Ben a 2.

"Mine anyway," Ben said.

The red and green pegs stood like proud soldiers on the cheap wooden cribbage board, ready to receive their marching orders.

Ben had a rather shitty hand. A, 3, 3, 4, 6, K. He decided to throw the 3's in his crib. He didn't know why some people called it a kitty. The game was not kittyage.

Darnell had a shitty hand as well. 2, 6, 8, J, Q, Q. He threw the 2 and 6 in Ben's crib, somewhat arbitrarily.

"Cut," Ben said. Darnell lifted half the deck, and Ben turned a 6 over and placed it on top. They were ready to roll.

Darnell placed his Queen. "Ten," he said.

"Sixteen," Ben said, as he laid his 6 down.

"Twenty-six," Darnell said, as he laid his other Queen.

Ben placed his 4. "Thirty."

"Go," Darnell said.

"Thirty-one," he said, and moved his green peg two points.

"Eight," Darnell said.

"Teen," said Ben.

Darnell threw down his Jack and took one point for the last card.

He counted his hand. "Two," he said, and took two points.

Ben counted his hand. "Fifteen-two and two is four." He took four points. He counted his crib. "Fifteen-two, fifteen-four, two is six, two is eight." He moved eight.

Darnell dealt the new hand. He looked at the cards he was holding. "Damn, I thought you took the Jokers out," he said to Ben.

"Oops," Ben replied.

Darnell flung his Joker across the room and pulled another card from the top of the deck. He was left with 3, 5, 7, 10, 10, Q. Not such a bad hand. He threw the 3 and the 7 in his crib.

Ben had A, 4, 6, 7, J, K. He threw the 4 and 7 to Darnell, then immediately cursed himself for breaking up his fifteens.

He cut the deck, Darnell drew a 2.

"Ten," Ben said, and put down a Jack.

"Fifteen," Darnell said, and placed a 5. He took two points.

"Twenty-one," Ben said.

"Are you feeling okay?" Darnell asked, as he put down a Queen. "Thirty one for two," he said, and moved his peg two points.

Ben placed a King. "Ten."

"Twenty," Darnell said.

"Twenty-one, fuck!"

Darnell smirked. "Thirty-one for three, ha!"

They counted their cards. Ben's pegs didn't move one bit.

"Fifteen-two, fifteen-four, fifteen-six, two is eight." Darnell advanced eight. He counted his crib. "One-two-three and two is five." He moved five.

"Do you even want to play?" he asked.

"Yes," Ben said.

"Because you're playing like a giant ass."

"I know," he said, and dealt.

He looked at his cards. "Son of a bitch!" he said. 3, 6, 7, 9, J, K. He threw the fifteen in his crib.

Darnell's cards: 4, 4, 9, 10, Q, K. He gave the Queen and 10 to Ben. Best to keep sure points. Now was not the time for risks.

He cut, and Ben flipped a King.

"Four," he said.

"Teen."

"Twenty-four."

"Thirty-one," Ben said, and moved two.

"Nine."

"Nineteen."

"Twenty-three."

"Twenty-six for the last card."

"Four," Darnell said, as he counted his hand.

"Two," Ben said. "And two in the crib."

Darnell dealt the new hand. A, 5, Q, Q, K, K. Not bad. He threw the two Kings in his crib.

Ben's cards: 3, 4, 7, 7, 8, J. He gave the 4 and 3 to Darnell. Ben cut; Darnell flipped a 7.

"Seven," Ben said, and put his 7 down.

"Teen," Darnell said.

"Twenty-seven," Ben said.

"Twenty-eight." Darnell.

"Go."

Darnell took a point.

"Eight." Ben.

"Teen," said Darnell.

"Twenty-five," said Ben.

Darnell threw down his last card and took a point.

Ben counted. "Fifteen-two, fifteen-four, fifteen-six and six is twelve." He took his points, which only put him three points ahead.

"Fifteen-two, fifteen-four, two is six here." Darnell said. "And two for the crib."

Ben gathered the cards and shuffled, and shuffled, and shuffled.

"Are you done?" Darnell asked.

"No," Ben said. "This time I'm getting a good hand."

"You got twelve," Darnell said.

"Not good enough," Ben replied. "I feel a twenty-nine coming on."

"Yeah," said Darnell. "Have you ever gotten a twenty-nine?"

"No."

But he was no longer paying attention to his moving hands, and the stiff cards flew in all directions, all over the floor.

"Fifty-two pickup!" Darnell shouted.

"That joke is lame!" Ben shouted back, and leaned over to pick the cards up.

One card, two cards, three cards. He picked them up one by one. He lifted his head to speak at Darnell. "You know, you..." He stopped his words. He caught a glimpse of something out the window. Just a glimpse. A shoulder. But it couldn't be. He was seeing things. Everybody was inside.

"Did you just see that?" Darnell said.

"Uh..." Ben replied.

"Did you just see somebody in the window?"

"Buh..." Ben replied, drooling.

"There was somebody out there," Darnell said for certain.

"I know," Ben said.

"Who do you think it is? Everyone's in here."

"I don't know," Ben said. "I'll go check it out."

"Good idea," Darnell agreed.

Ben walked to the back door and put his hand on the knob. He said a silent prayer to no god in particular, and opened the door a hair, just enough to stick his head out into the breezy night air.

"Hello out there!" he shouted. No answer.

"Hello?" he said again. "Who's out there?"

Nothing but the susurration of the crickets, peep frogs, and cicadas. Nothing but the hooting of a distant owl. Nothing but the snapping of fallen tree branches on the ground, most likely from an elk or caribou or platypus.

"Hello?" he shouted, only to be greeted by a distant echo of his voice.

He stepped outside the door. He could see very little beyond the shaft of light that spilled out of the door. Very little in the blackness of the backyard. And absolutely nothing in the treeline.

"Say, what's the meaning of this?" he asked whomever happened to be out there. But there was no reply. No noise at all, now. Or at least nothing that could be heard over the sound of slowly approaching footsteps.

Ben backed away slowly, keeping a useless eye in front of him, now wishing he had grabbed a weapon on his way out the door. A knife, a shovel, a TV Guide, anything. His heel hit the stoop and he almost toppled backwards. He regained his footing and walked through the door, the footsteps getting louder all the while.

He finally turned around and walked right into Floyd, whom he punched square in the gut, the force of air coming through his throat almost dislodging his epiglottis.

He slammed the door shut, but forgot to lock it, and as he was apologizing to Floyd for being such an inconsiderate prick, the door opened.

A lamb stood in the doorway. "Ba-a-a-a," it said.

"Oh, what a cute little..." Muffy began, and then screamed as the lamb's head fell from its neck and rolled onto the living room floor, its neck shooting blood in all directions, soaking the crowd.

36. The Guitar

Prostate cancer?

Is that what this was?

She didn't think so. For some reason it occurred to her that the prostate was in a different spot than the pain she was feeling now. For other, more mysterious reasons, it never occurred to her that she did not have a prostate.

The pain was coming from the front of her vagina.

Intense, yes, but it didn't start out that way.

It started as a much more mellow feeling in her goods, about an hour or so ago, and had since intensified.

Meanwhile, there was drama going on in other parts of the house. Judging by what she could overhear from her room, little bits heard through the small breaks in the monotonous tune that Doris was playing, apparently there was somebody outside.

Somebody outside, somebody not outside, it didn't matter to her right now.

No, it didn't matter to her at all, because her mind was slowly wrapping around what this lower body sensation was that was tearing her apart, little by little, until it fully dawned on her- PING:

She had to pee.

She had to pee like a bastard.

It made sense, now. The pain that started out as a mellow sensation. Increasing to sheer agony in the course of just an hour. It all made sense.

And it was funny, when she thought about it. Sometimes when she had to go, she knew it. More often than not, however, she ended up confused. And then each time when she solved the riddle, she remembered all the other times she had been confused about the bladder pain and had not been able to put two and two together. And she was fine, until the next time it happened, and she forgot all over again.

"I'll be back, yo," she said to her roommate, who shot her the finger-gun, which meant, *You do what you need to do. If you have to pee, if you have to poop, I'm there for you. And don't you ever think about killing yourself again, because I think I'm falling in love with you.* Okay, maybe it didn't mean all that.

She put her hand on the knob, turned it. She swung the door open and put one foot, two feet out into the hallway. She gently swung the door back to its fully closed position and took one step, two steps, three steps, four steps toward the bathroom door, on whose knob she put her hand on, turned, and swung open, only to put one foot in the room, two feet, and gently close the door. The commotion was still going on down-stairs- she thought she heard a sheep- but she couldn't care less.

She stood with her back to the toilet, preparing herself for a great relief. She undid the button on her pants, unzipped her fly, pulled down her pants and underwear, and sat on the cold porcelain seat.

She thought as the shudder ran through her quite feminine body how strange it was that porcelain was always cold. She remembered in her physics class when she learned that objects in and of themselves were neither hot nor cold. The sensation of heat or cold we got when we touched something was determined by the object's ability to absorb or reflect the room's heat, as well as your own body heat. Which did not go at all toward explaining the fact that no matter what time of year it was- it could be the hottest day in the middle of summer- a toilet seat was always a steady TWENTY degrees.

As her underthighs got used to the toilet's temperature, she relaxed a little. It took a while to get the flow started. She had waited so long that her muscles were in permanent lockdown. She cursed herself for waiting, but more often than not, that's what happened. Because she was always so confused, you see.

The urine started off with a slight trickle, then her muscles cinched up tight again, cutting off the flow.

"C'mon, Kiera. You can do this. You've done it before."

And she had done it before, yes. About 19,000 times before, so this should be no problem.

She took a couple of deep breaths and counted. "One...two...three...four..."

The trickle started. And ooh, boy, was that sweet relief. The sweet relief turned to sheer terror, however, as the urine began to shoot out of her like water from a fire hose. A steady jet of urine for a good full minute continued to shoot right into the toilet water, so much so that she could actually hear the water level actually draining on its own. A mixture of toilet water and pee splashed back up into her crotch, and man, was that cold. Much colder than the seat was.

And then, thankfully, the stream slowed down, until it was nothing more than a few loose dribbles shaking themselves free from her pee-hole.

The smell wafted upward, and soon was overpowering. Her pee often carried with it the stench of Cheerios. And usually it was a really dark amber color, too. Not clear- she would have even settled for yellow- but almost orange. She knew why. She knew she had to drink more water. She wasn't drinking any at the moment. In fact, in her lifetime she had tried water maybe a dozen times, and to her, it always tasted like shit. Even the bottled stuff. Her drinking habits mostly consisted of large amounts of Pepsi, and occasionally black coffee.

She took a small amount of toilet paper from the roll, just three squares. She wasn't sure what the acceptable amount of toilet paper was to use per wipe, but for her three squares was just enough. She wiped her naughty parts, front to back, as Oprah taught her to do, and her thumb knuckle mistakenly brushed against her urethra, soaking it in urine.

She cursed herself for being such a clumsy idiot, got up, and flushed the toilet. She pulled her pants back up, zipped and buttoned them, and looked at her thumb. Stained. A terrible shade of orange. She turned immediately to the sink and at once started scrubbing. After much effort her thumb was stain free, but try as she might, she couldn't completely get the smell of Cheerios out.

She shrugged, turned the faucet off, and headed out the door. She turned the knob, pulled it open, and stepped out of the bathroom. One step, two steps, three steps, four took her back to the bedroom. She put her hand on the knob, turned it, and opened the door.

And saw Doris, lying naked, face up in his bed.

Only it wasn't Doris. What was once Doris was now a new creation entirely. Six metal cords (were those his guitar strings???) had been screwed onto his hips, and ran all the way up his torso and into his mouth, which was much too gaping; his jaw must have been broken. Four bolts were sticking out of the side of his face, and two out of his ears. He looked a bit like a modern take on Frankenstein. Too literary for Kiera's taste.

But what was worse than all that, oh Lord have mercy, was his stomach. Someone had painstakingly carved a hole roughly the size of a softball. A perfectly symmetrical hole, and as she got close enough to see it in all its detail, she noticed that someone had completely hollowed him out.

Someone had turned Doris into an acoustic guitar.

Curiosity stronger than her disgust, she reached out and plucked the low E-string. It gave a nice twangggg! Not exactly pitch-perfect, but damn near close.

What the hell? she thought, and plucked it again. This time, however, she turned one of the keys. She tried the one that would normally correspond to that particular string, and for the love of Pete! It worked! It actually changed the sound of the string.

She turned and vomited on the floor. Okay, so maybe she *was* a little disturbed. She was in the bathroom for exactly two minutes and

FORTY-SEVEN seconds. How could somebody have done all this that quickly? It wasn't physically possible, and yet here it was.

And she noticed something else, too. Someone had wrote with lipstick down the sides of Doris, perhaps to add decoration. Perhaps to send a message. On one side was written: ENOUGH WITH THE GUITAR ALREADY, and on the other side, was written just one word: PING!

It occurred to her then: What if the killer was still in the house? What if the killer was still in the room, lurking in the closet? What if...

She collapsed.

37. The Shadowplay

It was too much; it was all too much. It was a little after two in the morning now, and Kiera just couldn't understand how the rest of the crew could sleep at a time like this. Everybody was dying. Everybody was getting slaughtered. And Doris, the worst one yet. And yet here they were, all sleeping.

It was too much; it was all too much. She gazed across the dark room at the empty bed there, and it was too much. After the guys had removed Doris' body from the room to add it to the heap that was getting bigger out back, they stripped the bed of all the sheets, even though there was surprisingly very little blood for such a gory scene. It was just a respect thing, she guessed. Respect for Doris, respect for Kiera, respect for the sanctity of the room, if there was any left.

She rolled over to face the wall. She didn't want to look at the bed anymore. But then she quickly became uncomfortable, lying with her back to the room. For all she knew, the killer could be standing right behind her.

She turned to face the room once again. Nobody there. But what if the killer was in the closet? Or under the bed?

Get a grip, Kiera. You're not going to get up and start searching everywhere like a paranoid. Just relax your mind for a while.

No. She couldn't relax too much, or she would drift off. She was not going to sleep. They only had a few more days here, and she would be damned if she would sleep through any of it. Perhaps she'd take a nap in the afternoon, when the rest of the house was up. But for now, she was on guard duty.

She watched the shadows of the trees play on the wall as the wind blew the branches back and forth. The moon was bright tonight. Not bright enough, however. Why couldn't it be bright enough to illuminate the whole room? Instead, it only caused the shadows. The creepy shadows. She felt like a little kid in a horror movie, just lying there staring at the shadows, thinking they were something they weren't. Like right now, she could swear she saw one shadow that looked like a person. That was impossible, however, since she was on the second floor.

Why, then, was there someone in the window?

She couldn't make out the face right away, but the more it stayed there, the more the branches of the trees moved back and forth, causing little shafts of moonlight to hit the face, one little fragment at a time, until she was finally able to piece it all together.

"Dad?" Kiera asked.

"Kiera? Kiera, honey, let me in," he pleaded.

She got up from her bed and raced to the window, never once thinking about the fact that her father had been dead for ten years.

"Dad, is that you?"

"Kiera. Sweetie. Open the window."

"What are you doing here?" she asked.

"They got me, honey," he said, not quite in answer to her question. "They got me," he repeated.

"Who got you?" she asked.

"So cold. It's cold here," he said.

"What do you mean, cold? It's the middle of summer," she said.

"Cold," he repeated, and shivered to prove his point.

She slowly turned the lock and opened the window.

NO! her mind screamed at her, and she quickly shut it again.

But it was too late. A much more powerful arm than hers had thrust itself between the window and the sill, and pushed the window back up.

She stood there for a moment, frozen to the spot, as she watched a person in a Michael Myers mask climb in the window like nobody's business. For all the originality the killer had shown thus far, there were definitely points lost on the mask. RUN, YOU FUCKING NIT! her mind screamed at her again, and she turned on her heels and fled. Before she made it two steps toward the bedroom door, it had its hold on her. She tried to scream, but before her brain could even calculate enough to do that, a cloth was held up to her mouth and nose.

She passed out for the second time that day.

The moonlight really is too bright, she thought, as her eyes came into focus. She immediately noticed that her mouth was sewn shut with what she thought was one of Doris' spare guitar strings. Her nostrils must have been glued together while she was out, as well. She could hardly breathe, except for the tiny little gaps between the stitches in her lips.

She didn't hurt right away; her head was swimming too much. But now the pain was coming to her, in slowly increasing waves.

And when the sheer agony was apparent on her face, her visitor stepped from the dark corner of the room to join her. Still wearing the mask, looking completely ridiculous. She didn't know why she thought it was her father out there; he had looked nothing like Michael Myers. Or William Shatner.

She had the sudden urge to scream as loud as she could; obviously her guest was being too quiet to alert the rest of the house.

"I see you're enjoying my little visit," the murdering bitch said. Or bastard. There was no telling the sex of the killer, as it spoke in an androgynous whisper.

"I know you're thinking of screaming and thrashing around and causing all kinds of a ruckus. You can if you want; I'm not going to stop you. And if you do, death will surely come for you, no questions asked. And once again I'll be forced to give you a chemical nap, and the next time you wake up you'll find yourself in a most precarious position. And no, I won't elaborate. Or you can be quiet and hold onto the hope that if you behave yourself and do as I ask, I may just let you go once I get my kicks. This is completely your decision and I stand by whichever one you make one hundred percent."

She pondered this for a moment, and stayed silent.

"I know earlier today you had a little spell. Feeling a little suicidal?"

She nodded.

"All because you didn't want to be in this position. Tortured. But your friends talked you out of it, didn't they?"

More nods.

"Just goes to show you, Kiera, that you should always choose the little voice inside you over your friends."

"Now let me see, here," her visitor said, as it rifled through a cute little attaché case. "Aah, yes. Here we go. You're gonna like this." It pulled what appeared to be a small wheel from the bag.

Pray tell, what are you going to do what that thing? she wanted to ask, but all that came out was, "Mrff."

"I'm glad you asked. Take a close look," the killer said, and held it right up close to her face. Yes, she'd recognized it, and it was more than just a wheel. Half the homes in America had one. A pizza cutter.

Give me a fucking break, she wanted to scream, but all that came out was, "Ffrm."

"Well, normally I couldn't agree more," the killer whispered. "But I spent quite a long time sharpening it. Gotta be able to cut through that thick pan pizza, you know? I mean, don't you hate it when you get a pizza home and they didn't cut it right, so you have to redo it?"

The blade was pushed against her skin, and it immediately sunk deep.

"See?" the killer asked, and she nodded.

"Well, you enjoy cutting yourself, right? How about eight equal slices?"

The killer made four long cuts across her bare torso. The blade, so thin and sharp, didn't really cause too much pain. Or bloodshed, for that matter.

"You know," it began, "those hideous scars you made all over your body, you really should have taken care of those. I'll let you in on a secret. Vitamin E. Put Vitamin E on those things and they'll fade a lot. Like this orange juice here," it said as it pulled a carton out of the bag, "has Vitamin E added." The visitor held the open carton over her. Kiera shook her head.

And the pain was horrible. Like nothing she had ever thought pain could feel like. Her senses were on fire.

But the killer quickly lost interest, as it went to the nightstand and retrieved something. Her journal. *You cocksucker!* she shouted in her head. *Put that down!*

It opened the book, and held it to the moonlight. It read the last poem Kiera wrote. It seemed to cry, but Kiera couldn't tell through the mask. The cry became laughter. "What a load of crap!" it said. "What a bunch of pretentious bullshit! I mean, get over yourself, already.

"You know," it continued, as it ripped the page out of her journal," I've always wondered if this would hurt." It took the sheet of paper and held it up to her eye.

Kiera attempted to shut her eyes before it could happen, then it occurred to her for the first time since she woke up that her eyelids were missing.

It ran the edge of the paper straight across her eye, making a nice thin papercut.

!!!

"I can tell by the look that there are indeed pain receptors in the eye. Good to know. Boy, you're a sight for sore eyes! Ha! Hold on, I've got something for that."

It shuffled through the bag again. "You know what's good for aches and pains? This stuff."

She didn't care. At this point she didn't know what was worse, the pain or having to endure this stupid session. The bad mask, the attaché, the constant rambling. Oh my God, it wouldn't shut the fuck up. *Shut the fuck up!* she wanted to yell.

"Here. You know what this is? Tiger balm. You can find it in your local drugstore. Good for aches and pains. Now, I know what you're thinking, Ben Gay is also good. Which is true. Can I let you in on a little secret? It's the same shit. But this is in a much smaller container. And it's more expensive. And it's got Chinese writing on it. And all those factors together make people think they're getting something much more effective than mentholated Vaseline. I know this is only good for muscles, but the eye is a muscle, so you never know," it said, and put a big gooey mentholated smear on both of her eyes.

!!!!!!!!!

"That hurts? Funny, I thought it would make them feel better. Sorry about that. Well, no sense in dwelling on it. Just think happy thoughts." It returned straight to the bag. It was picking up momentum now.

"How about this?" It said. "Doesn't this look like fun?"

Her eyes showed her nothing but blurs, like she was underwater, so she couldn't see what it was getting from its bag. Nor did she care. She just wanted it to be over so she didn't have to endure any more of the incessant rambling.

38. The Burning Bed

Knock knock knock.

"Who goes there?" Ben asked the closed bedroom door.

"It's me," he heard a female voice say from the other side.

"Me who?" he asked.

"You know who the fuck me who is," the voice said. Kiera.

"Well, can I come in?" she asked, impatient.

"You are always welcome in my boudoir," he answered.

"What's up?" he asked.

"Nothing. I just... I guess... I don't know."

"What is it?"

Her eyes welled up. "I miss Doris," she bawled.

"Oh, sweetie. Come here," he said, and patted the side of the bed he was not currently inhabiting.

She got up on the bed, laid her head on Ben's chest, and continued to cry. This was very unlike her, of course, but she had no control over it. Her tears were flowing by themselves, and it just felt so good to allow herself to be comforted for once.

"I mean," she said through sobs, "I know I only knew him for a few days, but I don't know; something happened between us. I just felt...connected...to him, you know? He was so nice to me. He talked to me, and I know how quiet he usually is. Ben, he knew my favorite songs. And to me, that meant more than anything. He always knew just what song to play for me. I know it sounds stupid, but I think I was starting to l-l-

Marc Richard

l-l..." the crying was just too great. She couldn't say the word. But when Ben silently mouthed, "Love him?" like the little pansy he was, she nodded.

"He used to say the sweetest things to me in between strums of his guitar," she said. "He told me that people love me. He told me I mean something in this world. It was the first time anybody said those kinds of things to me. And even though I didn't believe any of it, I still liked hearing it, you know?"

"Well, everything he said was true," Ben agreed.

Her head rose off from Ben's chest, and she looked him in the eyes. "And I'll tell you something else, too," she said. "He kissed me."

"He did?" Ben asked, not really shocked by it.

"Yeah," she said. "Just like this."

And before he knew it, her hands were rubbing his chest and her tongue was in his mouth.

It felt good. Ben hadn't kissed a girl like this since his girlfriend called their relationship off six months ago.

It felt right, somehow.

She pulled her mouth away from his and said, "And we made love, Ben. We didn't fuck. We made love. I'll show you."

"Well, I really don't think..." he began.

"I need to show you, Ben. I need to show you so you'll understand."

"Well, okay," he said. He couldn't argue with that. Maybe he did need to understand.

And before he knew it, his hands were rubbing her chest and his cock was inside of her.

And it felt good. It felt right. It felt...

Who the fuck was this?

"Uh, excuse me," Ben started. "But you have knuckles for a reason. Can't you knock?"

"Sorry," the guest whispered as it made its way inside the room. Kiera paid no attention to this.

150

She also paid no attention when the stranger approached the bed and began pouring kerosene all over them.

And she paid absolutely no mind when the match was struck and they were engulfed in flames.

"Excuse me," Ben began, but before long, the pain was so great he couldn't speak any more.

"Baaahhhh!" Ben screamed as he awoke from the dream, only to find himself surrounded by flames. He thought of getting up from the bed, but he couldn't move.

Floyd came into the room, followed by Chet, still half-asleep.

"Holy shee-yit!" Floyd yelled.

Chet stood there like a dumb chicken for a minute, till Floyd said, "Blankets. We need blankets," and they both raced out of the room to grab their blankets and sheets off the bed.

The fire continued to rage; raging.

The fire continued to burn; burning.

The drapes dangled dangerously close to the burning raging flames, but the drapes were not interested in catching fire today.

Ben was not yet on fire, however, his skin was starting to sizzle from the sheer heat.

Running back into Ben's room, Floyd said, "Ready?"

Chet nodded.

"Go!" Floyd said, and at Go they both threw their blankets and sheets on Ben, successfully smothering the flames.

"Ow," Ben squeaked.

Slowly, Chet pulled the sheets back to reveal to himself a sight which he had never seen before.

The sight of a broiled human being.

Ben resembled a Thanksgiving turkey. It looked as though his skin would just break and flake off with a crispy snap if you touched him.

"Oh my God," Chet said. "What do we do?"

Floyd just stared dumbly.

Ben sighed, annoyed that he had to do the thinking for these two panic-stricken yahoos when he could barely form a coherent thought himself through all the pain.

"There's a bucket," he croaked. "Under the kitchen sink." He took a few panting breaths. It felt as though he had breathed the fire in and seared his lungs. Perhaps it was the smoke he inhaled; he didn't know, but he continued. "Fill with cold water."

Floyd followed direction and trudged downstairs.

"Excuse me," he said, as he made his way past Darnell and the twins, who were headed upstairs.

"What's that smell?" Darnell asked.

"Ben's room," was all Floyd could think to say.

"Oh my God!" Floyd heard Darnell say.

"Blllarrrgghhh!" he heard one of the twins vomit. He couldn't blame her. He didn't know which was worse, the sight of Ben or the smell of burnt flesh, which now seemed to be wafting through the entire house.

A knock on the front door. Floyd turned from the sink and looked at the time. 2:30. Who the hell could be knocking on the door at 2:30 a.m.? He stared at the front door, frozen, the bucket runnething over.

Knock knock knock again. Floyd's gaze turned once again to the clock on the microwave. 2:31. The killer. They were all gonna die. And he was next, since he was closest to the front door.

Another knock, only this time it was followed by a, "Hello? Is anybody home?"

This was not the voice of the killer. Floyd knew right away whom this young-sounding voice belonged to. Thawed out from his trance, he shut the water off and took the bucket out of the sink.

He put it down by his feet and flung the door open wide.

Yep, he was right. Standing there, looking slightly confused and a little more annoyed, was the pizza delivery guy.

"Hey, yer late," he informed the youngster. "I called like eight hours ago. Don't I git it free?"

The boy just looked into Floyd's eyes with an *Oh no, you didn't just say that* stare.

"They sent me out here in the middle of nowhere. I am way outside of my delivery radius. Your address doesn't exist in my GPS system, let alone Mapquest. It's 2:30 in the morning. I'm tired. I'm hungry. And you're goddamned lucky I didn't just say fuck it and pull over and eat both of these fucking pizzas and turn around and go home. Now, do you want these or not? Because I'm about ready to break the cardinal rule and cross this threshold. And after I do that, I'm going to beat the fucking piss out of you and make my own pizza out of your fat, doughy ass. Whaddaya say?"

Floyd threw his hands up in surrender. "Okay, okay. I was jist jokin' anyways."

He reached into his front pocket and pulled out a crumpled wad of greenbacks. "How much do I owe you?"

"NINETEEN dollars," the kid said. "And FORTY-THREE cents."

"Jeezit Cripes, they don't give these things away. Here." He said, and handed a wad of cash to the boy, slightly damp from being in Floyd's front pocket, right next to his sweaty crotch. "Keep the change."

"Uh, okay," the kid said. "There's, like, eighty-five dollars here," he informed him.

"Keep it," Floyd instructed. "I ain't go no mo use for it anyways."

"Thanks," the kid said. "Hey, what's that smell?"

Floyd slammed the door shut.

"What took you so long?" Chet asked as Floyd gallumphed his way into the room.

"I brought the water," Floyd said, not answering the question.

"It's too late now," Buffy said, carefully touching Ben. "His skin's already cool."

"What took you so long?" Chet asked again.

"Look what I got," Floyd said, sounding like an eight-year-old.

"Is that...?" Darnell asked.

"Yep. Pizza," he confirmed. "I ordered it before you caught on fire," Floyd said as he opened the boxes up. "Sorry if it reminds you of your face," he told Ben.

Ben almost felt like punching Floyd right in his fat stomach, but let out a big guffaw instead. Soon he was laughing so hard he didn't think he could stop.

The rest of the gang started chuckling, and soon it sounded like Friday night at the Comedy Connection.

"Heh-heh-ha-ha-ha," Ben chortled. "Get the salve."

39. The Afterthought

H ey," Darnell interrupted in the midst of all the munching and laughing and festivities, "aren't we missing someone?"

Suddenly, Ben remembered the dream he had. He had a bad feeling. A really bad feeling. "Oh, no," he chirped.

Chet looked at Floyd. Floyd looked at Darnell. Darnell looked at Ben. Ben looked at Muffy. Muffy looked at Buffy. Buffy looked at Chet. Chet looked at Darnell. Darnell looked at Muffy. Muffy looked at Ben. Ben looked at Floyd. Floyd looked at his feet, then quickly up at Chet, hoping Chet didn't notice. Luckily, Chet was too busy looking in the mirror, watching himself saying, "Well, I'm not going to go in there," as he hooked a thumb toward the bedroom across the hall. Or what he thought was the bedroom across the hall, but since he was so busy admiring himself, his thumb inadvertently ended up pointing straight at Floyd's ass.

"And I ain't gonna let you in there," Floyd answered.

This received a teeny, "Ha," from Buffy.

"Quiet down, Bertha, for all we know you could be the killer," Chet exclaimed.

"Are you fucking serious? How would I be capable of doing the things that the killer has done? You're mental. If anyone's capable of that shit it's you. I mean, look at the facts. You're a strong guy. You're fucking tweaked. You're always the first to sling accusations. To deflect some of the suspicion, maybe? Not to mention I think you might be gay."

"You think so?" Muffy said. "You know, I had a feeling that the night we shared together was his first time. And he didn't really seem into it, did he?"

"No," Buffy agreed, "he didn't."

"Well, what about Floyd?" Chet said, choosing to ignore the last few seconds of the conversation completely.

"What about me?" Floyd asked.

"Whuuttt abowwtt muheeee?" Chet poorly imitated. "You're just as capable as anybody else. You're an outsider. You don't belong here. With your stupid backass podunk ways. Why don't you go the fuck back to Alatucky or Kentuckabama or wherever it is you're from?"

"Georgia."

"Jee-orr-gee-uh. You redneck. It's obvious you're the killer."

"Maybe you're the killer," Darnell chimed in.

"For the love of Pete, would you all just shut the fuck up!?! Ow." Ben said. Talking made every nerve in his body ache, he wasn't sure why. But yelling the way he just did was pure agony. "We've been over this a million times. I'm tired of hearing it. We all know it's none of us. Any moron can see that. We need to stop this. It's a waste of time. Just stop. Let's enjoy the time we have together, as short as it may be. And somebody needs to go check on Kiera."

"Fine," Chet relented. "I'll go."

...

"Oh my God!"

Ben closed his eyes when he heard the shout. It was becoming too routine.

Chet rushed back into Ben's room. "Guys, you have to come see this. You'll never guess what he did this time."

And one by one, they all reluctantly filed in. All except for Ben, who couldn't move. And one by one, their jaws all dropped when they saw the sight that lay before them.

"Well, the killer is certainly getting creative. Jesus Christ."
It was a sight not meant for the eyes of the sane.

40. The Infection

Knock knock knock.

Ben awoke from his sweet dreams with a strong sense of déjà vu. He didn't know why- he couldn't recall when the last time was that he awoke from a dream burnt to a crisp from his bed being on fire the night previous.

He painfully turned his head and looked at the clock on the nightstand. 3 p.m. Was that even possible? Could he have slept almost twelve hours, considering the pain he was in? Perhaps his body had gone into a nice peaceful state of shock. He tried to look down at his body, but when his head tried to aim in that direction, it caused his singed neck to tense right up in severe agony. Forget it. It was probably best he didn't look anyway.

Knock knock knock. Oh yeah. "Come in," he said, hoping to God it wasn't the killer he just told to come in. Then again, would the killer have knocked? He didn't think so. No, something told him the killer was not a knocker, but rather a barger-inner.

The door opened surreptitiously.

"You don't have to open the door surreptitiously," Ben called. "I know you're at the door. You just knocked."

"Oh yeah," Darnell said as he let himself in. "Hey, I just wanted to see how you were..." His sentence was cut short and his eyes bugged so far out of his head that he was sure they were going to jump right out of his face and hail a cab the fuck out of there. "...doing."

"Is it that bad?" Ben asked. Stupid. Of course it was that bad.

Darnell stared at Ben's naked charred body. It certainly didn't look good. In fact, it looked worse than it did when they left him to rest this morning. But what was he going to say? He didn't want to crush Ben's spirits, but where giant sheets of flesh had fallen off of his body like a blanket, there were now what appeared to be giant pus-filled sores. The remaining flesh was no longer the pink color of freshly cooked human meat. It was now mostly brown, and in spots it looked like it was turning a hint of green.

"Well, I...uh..."

"Tell me straight, man. Tell me the truth."

"Well, dude, you don't look at all...healthy."

"I'm sure I don't."

"I think everything's starting to get all...infected."

"Really?"

"Yeah, you're starting to pus, it looks like. It...it...it doesn't look good, dude."

"Fuck. How could I be getting so infected already?" he asked Darnell, as though he were a doctor.

"I don't know. If we had found the salve or something..."

"I swore to God we had some."

"I found this in Kiera's room," Darnell said. "Do you think it'll help? It's sort of salvey."

"Tiger Balm? No, I think that would do more harm than good."

"Well, I don't know what to say, man. Can I get you anyth..."

BANG!!! CRASH!!! Peter Paul and Mary THUD!!!

"Da fuck?" Darnell asked.

"Sounded like it was coming from the attic," Ben said.

"It's...him."

Ben noticed something odd at that moment. Instead of looking frightened, as he should be, Darnell appeared to be, well, pissed.

"That's it. I've had it. I'm going to put a stop to this once and for all. Or die trying. Bonsai, motherfucker!" he shouted as he hurled himself from Ben's bedroom.

41. The Flashlight

The creaking and cracking the collapsible attic stairs made as he was climbing them reminded him of little sticks and twigs in his fairytale imagination. Darnell had no idea what that meant, and if he had heard me narrating like this, he probably would have applied a kick to my groin area.

There was no telling how long it had been since somebody had been up here, but judging by the amount of cobwebs that were stringing all over his face, it had been quite a while. Man, it was dark. Even though it was the afternoon, the meager amount of daylight getting through the vents cut on either end of the attic wasn't doing shit. Ben said there was a light up here, but he brought his flashlight just in case it had burnt out, which it had. It probably would have made for a much better lighting situation if he'd just taken the bulb out of any of the light fixtures downstairs and replaced this one with it, but whatever.

"Hello?" He called stupidly. "Is anybody up here?"

He trained the long silver flashlight with its weakening beam in all directions. It would have made sense if he had taken the batteries out of his radio and replaced these ones with those, but aren't we just splitting hairs at this point?

The flashlight strained really hard to capture the entire room in its light beam, but it couldn't muster enough strength. That's personification, folks.

"Damn," he said as more cobwebs and shit attacked him. He tried wiping off his face and arms, but it seemed to just create more problems. He was getting irritated, and the more irritated he became, the jumpier he became.

Darnell stood still for a moment, trying to calm his nerves. He listened intently for any sign of the noise he heard earlier.

Wait

wait

wait

nothing.

All was quiet up here. No thumping, no banging, no shuffling. And all that meant absolutely nothing. There were no windows up here. No means of escape. And the only way down would have been these stairs. There was no way anyone could have come down these stairs and folded them back up into the ceiling in the time it took him to grab the flashlight from the hall closet.

"Hello?" he called again. Man, he was just begging for it. If nobody was up here waiting to kill him, there ought to be.

He walked a little further into the dark recesses of the attic, realizing at once that this was only the kind of stupid move that you saw in horror movies. In real life, if you felt that someone was in your attic, you got the fuck out of the house. Strangely, though, he felt no compulsion to do that. The desire to put an end to this mess once and for all was just as strong as it had been before he came up here.

Even further into the attic he went, shining his still fading beam of light to the left, to the right. Completely ignoring what was right in front of him, however. He tripped. Over what, he had no idea. It was a long fall, and as he was going down, he noticed something moving over to the right.

"Guff!" A big puff of air escaped him as he landed flat on his stomach. The flashlight was sent spinning out of control.

He was completely winded, but he couldn't take too long to recover. He had to find the flashlight and figure out what the hell was up here with him, before whatever was up here with him discovered him.

Darnell got up on his knees, and started crawling and pawing in the darkness. The torch couldn't have gone too far. It must have rolled under something. It shouldn't be too hard to find; the light was probably still on. Dim as it was, he should be able to locate it.

His hands shuffled in the darkness, gathering the fine blanket of dust that had settled on the wooden attic floor. He was going to have to sneeze in a second if he kept this up. He hoped he could stave off the urge to sneeze, though- he didn't want to reveal himself.

Don't want to reveal yourself? he thought. Don't be retarded, it's a little too late for that.

Search, search, search. Meanwhile, he could hear movement coming from his right. Oh, where the fuck is that thing?

His hands stumbled upon something. What is that? A boot? Oh God. His hand swung out in front of him and touched the light. So it *had* gone out. He quickly picked it up and slid the thumb switch up. Nothing. Oh shit. Had it gasped its last amount of energy? He slid the switch down and up again, shaking it violently. It came back on; a little stronger than before, actually. Go figure. He quickly shined the beam at the boots. There were no feet in them. Just boots. Whew!

He got up and with much trepidation walked over to the right. There was something moving there, slightly, underneath what appeared to be a rather large green tarp.

"Come on out of there," he said to the shape. "I'm tired of your bullshit. You can't hide."

It suddenly appeared in his little mind that he had armed himself with absolutely nothing. He hoped beyond hope that the flashlight was heavy enough to bash somebody's skull in without giving, because it was too late to turn back.

His arm reached slowly out to the tarp. He grasped it tightly, and counted to three.

"One..."

He grabbed the vinyl even tighter.

"Two..."

His other hand grasped the flashlight tighter, ready to strike. His tarp arm tensed as he poised himself to pull it back like a magician pulling the tablecloth out from under the fine china.

"Three..."

And revealed their visitor, lying in wait.

Darnell screamed like a girl.

The killer sprung up out of his chair, put his hands around Darnell's neck and began to choke the life from his young body.

He struggled to fight back, beating upon the killer's head with the flashlight, but the man was relentless. Darnell escaped his own body and watched with a vague interest as his life was fading away.

Of course, this was all in his own mind; I believe I told you at the beginning that he had a fairytale imagination.

Nobody was choking him. There was no killer.

No, but there was someone in the chair. A woman. Was that the killer's latest victim? Not a victim yet, as she was still moving. Who was this woman?

"Ma'am?" he asked. "Ma'am are you all right? Ma'am? Answer me, dammit!"

He gave her a smack across her mouth, which happened to be frozen in a rictus, and that's when he realized, This woman wasn't real. She was made of vinyl, not unlike the tarp she had been under.

Darnell couldn't stand it. All of this build up and suspense for an inflatable sex doll. He roared. This was fucking hilarious. She must have been deflating a little, and that was the movement.

"Well guys," he said to no one. "I guess I deflated her." And that sent him into hysterics. This was about the funniest thing he had ever seen.

And he noticed, through the laughter, a very peculiar cardboard sign hanging around her neck.

DREW'S PLAN A

were the words on the sign, written in Sharpie. He had no idea what that meant, but it made him laugh even harder.

Good times.

42. The Path

Floyd heard Darnell scream like a girl over the television that was blasting downstairs. They all did. He did not hear the hysterical laughter that soon followed, as he didn't stick around long enough to hear it.

"That's it. I had it."

And with that, he stormed out of the house, out the back door and was never heard from again.

Floyd went to the edge of the lot past his dead friends' bodies and started down the only trail that led away from here. He needed to get away. There was no way he was ever going back to that house. He didn't know why he had stuck around so long, but it didn't matter at this point why. He just had to get as far away from there as possible. He wasn't quite sure if he'd ever get back to civilization, but he'd be damned if he wouldn't die trying. He sure as hell wasn't going to sit around and wait to die like the rest of them. Fuck them. Fuck them all.

He knew that going out the front door and down the road was certainly the most obvious choice, and that was perhaps why he didn't take it. He didn't trust the road. Too many bad things happened on the road. His mind flashed back to the dead teenagers, and the semi truck speeding through with no one at the wheel.

As he was walking past Chet's unnecessarily large woodpile, he ruminated on the many reasons why there would be a path like this through the woods. One possibility, and the one he had hoped, was that it led to another camp. It seemed like there were quite a few in this area; some of them even appeared to be inhabited. Not on Harm's Way, of course, where everyone was dead, but farther down the road, closer to town.

Town? There was no town. The closest town probably took two days by foot, and in his fat shape it would take him even longer.

Another reason for the path was maybe it was a snowmobile trail. He knew that those trails always led somewhere eventually, but he'd seen snowmobile maps before, and to him they always looked like a road map would look on Mars. Yeah, they led somewhere, but there were sometimes a hundred miles or more of nowhere in between two somewheres. If this was the case, as it could very well be up here at the Canadian border, he was doomed. He couldn't huff a hundred miles by foot. He'd drop dead of a heart attack before he ever got to that point. His hope was dwindling.

But wait. What was that up ahead? Was that?

Could that be?

A house?

Yes, it most certainly was a house. He could see the roof winking through the trees, beckoning him to come near.

He started running. He ran as far as his fat body would carry him, which was about fifty feet, but it was enough to realize that something didn't seem right about this house.

Something seemed very...familiar.

A few more steps and he realized why. He was right back where he started. What the fuck? He'd been walking for a good half hour or so only to get absolutely nowhere.

A few more steps and he saw a shape.

A human shape. One that was not recognizable. A human shape wearing, of all things, a mask from that horror movie. Was it Freddy Kruger? He didn't really know his horror movies too well, because he was a good Southern Baptist, but he knew them well enough to give him

167

a clue that this person meant no good. There was no mistaking it. This was the killer.

He turned and ran back into the woods as far as his fat body would carry him, which was about fifty feet, and chanced a look back over his shoulder. The killer was just standing there. Not giving chase or anything. It was almost as though he didn't register Floyd's presence at all.

He had to keep walking. After about five minutes of walking, the path forked. He hadn't noticed that before, so which way did he go? It was most probable that he went to the left, since it seemed the straighter of the two. So this time he went right.

That must have been the right choice. The path didn't seem familiar to him at all. This didn't give him the warm fuzzy feeling he was expecting, however, for the simple fact that it seemed to be disappearing.

The farther he walked, the less it seemed like a path, until he was suddenly deep in the woods. But what could he do at this point? He couldn't very well turn around and head back, walking toward the killer. No, every step back was, well, a step back.

So on he trudged, deeper and deeper into the woods, and when it seemed that all hope was lost he came into a clearing.

A clearing with a very familiar looking camp.

Oh, come on!

And there, at the edge of the yard, was the killer, who was now sitting in a lounge chair, yawning. As if he were bored of watching this.

Well, what the hell? Floyd thought as he walked through the woods back to the path once more. He headed back into the woods. Now it was only a matter of time, he thought. There was no way out of here. He obviously wasn't cut out for hiking. He had absolutely no bearings.

He shot another look over his shoulder, and this time his worst fears were justified. The killer finally got up and started following him. He was giving chase.

Albeit a very slow chase. Floyd wanted to run. He wanted so badly for adrenaline (which has been since renamed "epinephrine" by scientists. Why do they insist on renaming shit?) to kick in and run like the wind. But he no longer had it in him. Scared? Yeah, he was scared to death, but not enough to-

"Huh?" he said as he was whapped in the back with something. He stopped walking for a second and looked down. A beer bottle. The killer was taunting him. He could easily catch up to him and end it right now, but he didn't want to. He wanted to prolong this and make this as fun as possible. Something in Floyd told him to just beg for mercy and ask to be killed. But a bigger something told him he was fucking stupid for even thinking that.

So he pressed forward, further on the path, until an object whizzed by him.

He knew a pitchfork when he saw one. The killer was strong. He threw that pitchfork like a baseball. Not much aim, though.

He reflected on a time, he supposed he was about FIVE or so, when his daddy bought him his first shotgun and took him out shooting pumpkins. He could barely hold the gun up, so of course he missed the target. "You couldn't hit the broad side of a barn door with a bushel basket," paw told him. That was the only time when he thought about shooting paw and gunning the whole family down. He was glad he didn't. And he did finally become a better shot.

He laughed to himself. Was it right to be scared of someone who couldn't hit the broad side of a barn door with a bushel basket? What was there to be scared of? Obviously this guy wasn't infallible. He had flaws. He almost thought of turning around and facing the killer when he got pinged in the back of the head with something very large and very hard. "Jesus Christ," he exclaimed. The Lord would forgive him, given the circumstances. He looked down, and through the stars that were swimming before him, he saw a frozen turkey lying on the ground.

He looked back at the killer. "Oh, come on," he said.

The killer just shrugged.

Floyd trudged on, followed closely behind, and almost took a right at another fork when a rock whizzed by his head. The killer had obviously run out of objects to throw.

He turned around and saw the killer shaking his head. He pointed straight down the road. This reminded Floyd of a scene from some movie. He wasn't sure which one it...

But when he saw the stone in the path and the mound of dirt piled next to a large hole he remembered the movie right away. A Christmas Carol, by that blasphemer, Charles Dickens. This stone was a grave marker, a headstone. He knew what the stone would say before he even looked at it.

FLOYD COOT

This was meant for him.

"Gee, it must have taken you a long time to do this," he said.

The killer just shrugged, as if to say, *Yeah, but what else do I have to do? It's no big deal, really.*

"So I s'pose I gotta get in this."

The killer nodded.

"I s'pose there's no negotiatin'"

The killer shook his head.

There was no use arguing anymore. Floyd did as he was told and got in the grave.

And a strange calm washed over him as the dirt rained down.

43. The Deal

Hey, it's…" Chet turned his attention from the TV and said "5:02," like that meant something.

"Yeah, I can read time," Muffy said back.

"Hey. I'll make a deal with ya," he said.

"Oh? What?"

"Why don't you go see if you can find my roommate?"

…

…

…

…

…

…

…

"And???" she said, impatiently.

"And what?"

"And what will you do?"

"Do? I'm doing what I do," he said in an obvious tone.

"Well, I thought a deal was a trade," she said.

"It is," he said.

"So what will you do?" she asked.

"Fine, I'll go check on Ben," he answered.

"You know," her sister butted in, "that's not much of a deal. Maybe she'd like to go check on Ben. I'd like to check on him myself."

"So go," he said.

"Then you can go find Floyd," Buffy said.

"That wasn't the deal," Chet said.

"THERE WAS NO DEAL!" she answered.

"Fine. You wanna go look at Ben, all skinless and missing half his flesh, you can. I'll wait down here while I listen to you puking your guts out like you did earlier."

"He needs tending to, Chet. He's not well. And I care about him, Chet. Maybe, Chet, you don't know what that's like, being so hollow and empty, Chet. I'm going to see how he's doing out of the kindness of my heart, Chet, not because I want to make some stupid deal. Chet."

"Do what you want. It's a free country," Chet said.

"Damn right it is. So why don't you go find your roommate?"

"No."

"Yeah, you don't want to. Who does? He's been gone for almost two hours, now. He's not out for a stroll. He's not coming back. He's dead. DEAD! There's no sense in going to look for him because he's fucking dead!"

"Excuse me," she said to Darnell as he came down the stairs.

"Yo Darnell," Chet said vernacularly. "Floyd's ran off into the woods. You wanna go find him?"

"Bonsai, motherfucker!" he yelled and fled out the door.

Chet shook his head. He'd heard Darnell yell it the first time, and that was enough. Bonsai, motherfucker! is not an expression that should be used more than once in a day.

"Well, I hope you're happy," Buffy said. "We'll never see Darnell again."

"Go check on Ben," he blurted, and turned his attention back to the TV. "Oh, and while you're up there, fiddle-fucking around, why don't you see if you can find the poor guy some salve."

Her foot stopped dead on the stair, and her head whipped around. "Screw you, Chet!" she yelled. "You know damn well there's no salve! Come on, Muffy, let's go."

And Chet heard the knock on Ben's door.

And Chet heard Ben's door open.

And Chet heard one of the twins vomit. Most likely Muffy. It was priceless.

"Sorry about her," Buffy said to Ben. "She's just got a weak stomach."

"It's okay," Ben said, in a raspy voice. "I know I'm repulsive."

"Oh, you're not that bad," she said.

But he was. And if Buffy had seen him a couple of hours ago, she'd know that he'd gotten a lot worse since then. The skin was gone completely from his body, and more flesh was sloughing off by the minute. Big layers of muscle tissue had started to break open much like a quake will crack the earth's crust, just from the sheer force of the fluids bursting free.

"Are you in pain?" she asked.

"Agony," he replied.

"What's wrong with your voice?"

"I don't know," he gurgled. I assume the infection has moved into my lungs." And as if to prove this point, he hocked up a stinky green bile the likes of which she had never seen in any of her medical journals.

"I can't believe there's no salve," he said.

"Sorry sweetie. We looked."

"Oh, well. Can you help? I'm sticking to the bottom sheet. Just un-bunch it from my skin."

Skin? she thought. What skin? But she did as he asked. The sheet came away from his body with a crusty tearing sound that was nauseating.

Muffy vomited again.

All was not well. Her friend was dying.

44. The Burial Site

He stood there, staring. He couldn't believe it.

FLOYD COOT

And fresh dirt, too. Buried alive.

It couldn't be. This had to be some sort of sick joke.

But something was telling him it wasn't. This was real.

Floyd was under here.

Coot??? You gotta be fucking kidding.

Water started to spew forth from his tear ducts. He headed back to camp, sorry he was going to have to break the news to the rest of the gang. He had actually started to like Floyd. Poor Floyd.

He stopped dead in his tracks.

Wait! What time was it? He didn't know, but it was probably around 5:30. And how long had Floyd been missing? That was an even bigger question. Maybe a couple of hours.

Could it be possible, then, that Floyd was still alive? Maybe, if he had enough airspace...

Could anyone stay buried that long?

He didn't know; he wasn't an expert on live burials, but he thought maybe, just maybe, he had a shot. It was worth a try, anyway.

He went back to the dirt mound. He thought about stamping on it, but thought he'd better not. If there were any air pockets left, that was sure to fill them with dirt.

He had no choice, then. He had to shout, and perhaps attract the attention of anyone that may be out here.

Suddenly, he wasn't feeling that same bravado he'd felt just two hours ago up in the attic. He wasn't ready to die.

But Floyd, dammit! Do it for him!

All right, fine. "FFLLOOOOYYYYD!"

He bent down, put his ear to the ground, and waited.

"mmffeffll," he heard coming from below. So he was alive! But judging by the distant sound of Floyd's yell, he was a long way down.

"Don't worry, buddy! I'll get you out!"

But how? With what? He couldn't dig him out by hand. He'd thought about the random objects lying in the path he'd followed to get here. The beer bottle wouldn't work. The frozen turkey wouldn't work. The pitchfork may work, but it would take a while. His only option was to go all the way back to camp and look for a shovel.

He looked down the path. If he ran all the way to the house, he could be there and back in ten minutes. But how long would it take him to find a shovel? He might have to go upstairs and ask Ben, rather than waste time searching blindly, like they all had done with that damned salve. But that would take up even more time.

And he had wasted even more time, standing here thinking about it. Well, no time like the present, man. Go! Go! Go!

Darnell took off as fast as his legs would carry him. He hoped this all wasn't for nothing. If they had no shovel, he'd have to run back and start digging with the pitchfork. Ten minutes he would waste, for nothing. His mind was searching for any reason why they would have a shovel at camp. Did Ben and his mom ever come here in the wintertime? But that didn't matter; a snow shovel was not a digging shovel. He needed a spade.

The irony was not lost on him, either, but he didn't really have time to laugh about it. A black man looking for a spade. He should kick his own ass for even thinking that it was mildly funny, and goddammit all this thinking was probably slowing him down.

Oh, shit, what was that? But why bother asking yourself that question you fucking idiot you know damned well what that is and he's right behind you.

Run, Darnell! Run!

And he did. He ran. And he knew it would slow him down, but he had to chance a look over his shoulder, just to confirm his fear. Yep, there the killer was, wearing a stupid Michael Myers mask and giving a pretty decent chase.

He guessed he was probably halfway back to the camp when he stumbled, and hit the ground hard. His mind flashed back to the spill he took in the attic. Not again, Lord. Not again. Broken and bruised, he could not afford the time it took to get his bearings back this time, or to get the air back in his lungs. He got right back up and stared running again. Or attempted to, but he realized very soon that he could not when a jolt of pain shot through his leg. He looked down. There was a rather large lump on his leg. He reached down and felt it. Yep, that was bone. It had not made its way through his skin, but he knew for sure that it was broken.

The pain was so unbearable that he almost didn't care when the killer had finally caught up with him.

The killer was panting. However, not so out of breath that there wasn't enough strength to hoist a big boulder up high in the air and hold it over Darnell's head.

"Holy moley," Darnell panted. "That thing must weigh three hundred pounds. Where do you get the strength?"

"adrenaline," the killer said weakly. The strength was fading. But it was epinephrine now.

"I wanna thank you," Darnell said.

"for what?" the killer barely squeaked out.

"For not killing the brother off first."

The stone dropped, and sheer agony pierced through his skull as it became nothing but a stain on the dirt floor.

45. The Chickenshit

K ids, umm, it's midnight," Chet once again made his astute observations.

"Yeah, I can read time," Muffy said back.

"Way I see it, Darnell's been gone an awfully long time. Where do you suppose he is?" Chet asked.

"Where do I suppose he is?" Buffy repeated. "He's dead. He's fucking dead. Where the hell do you think he is? He's dead, for God's sake. And it's all your fault."

"My fault? Why my fault?"

"You sent him out there to look for Floyd, who was also obviously dead, rather than just go yourself," Buffy said.

"But then I'd be dead," Chet said.

"I don't see a bad side to that, necessarily."

"Yowza."

"And what really pisses me off, you tried to send her."

"Yeah," Muffy said.

"And if you actually convinced her to go and she came up missing, so help me God I'd kill you myself."

"All right, look," Chet began. "It's late; we're tired. Nobody's thinking rationally here. Let's all get some sleep and maybe we'll figure this all out in the morning. Good night, ladies."

"Go fuck yourself, Chet," Buffy shouted as Chet headed upstairs to his room.

"Hey, you awake?" Muffy said to Buffy.

"Yeah," Buffy said.

"I can't sleep," Muffy said.

"Me either." Buffy.

"Well, do you want to play a game or something?" Muffy.

"Sounds good to me." Buffy.

"What do you want to play?" Muffy.

"I don't know." Buffy.

"Well, there are, like, FORTY-FOUR games in the downstairs closet. Go get something and we'll play." Muffy.

"Down...stairs?" Buffy asked.

"What, are you scared or something? Come on, Buffy. Don't start being a chicken now. I rely on you to be strong. There's nobody down there that'll harm you. Everybody that was sleeping down there is dead."

"That's comforting."

But she went, anyway, the brave girl. And when Muffy finally heard her sister's feet hit the bottom step, she leapt out of her sofa bed and she was gone. She couldn't take it anymore. She needed to get out. She needed a safe place. Muffy hoped to God that her sister would be all right, but right now she had to do what she felt she had to do.

Off to the outhouse she went, again.

Everyone was dead. Muffy contemplated the magnitude of what that meant, as much as she could contemplate magnitude. Wasn't very easy for her to do, since her sister got all the brains. For the most part, she was good at doing just one thing: Looking pretty. So usually she'd be brushing her hair or applying her makeup while her sister would be busy contemplating magnitude.

To tell you the truth, and I may as well tell the truth to you. There is not sense in hiding anything from you at this point, is there? I mean, besides who the killer is, but maybe you'll figure it out. These losers sure as hell aren't going to. Truth is something that is hard to come by nowadays, but before I start to get on a political rampage, let me stop myself. This is not the time nor the place. Now, where was I?

Oh, yes.

To tell you the truth, Muffy was always a little jealous of her sister. Sure, she was the prettier twin. But she was prettier in an indefinable, I-can't-quite-put-my-finger-on-it kind of way. And Buffy, well, she was also quite stunning, and smart. It seems like Buffy got eighty percent of the brains, and she still ended up with FORTY-FIVE percent of the looks.

She was jealous, yes, but not to the point of resenting her. No way. She would die for her sister. She would throw herself in front of a run-away train for her sister. She would jump in front of an out-of-control Macy's Thanksgiving Day balloon for her sister. She would eat a whole plate full of shit just to keep her sister from smelling it. That's what she would do for her sister.

Then why aren't you with her right now, Muffy? Because all of those other things were in the abstract, and when it came right down to it, she knew damn well she was not brave enough to do any of those things. And at this moment, she felt, the best way to help Buffy was to help herself.

"I couldn't help but read your thoughts," a voice came from the toilet-hole.

Before she knew it, the killer had climbed up and out of the toilet-hole. How did it happen so quickly? She'd never seen anyone climb so fast out of a toilet-hole before. She didn't even have time to register the fact that she should be pissing her pants right now.

"You're wondering about your sister," the killer said.

Actually, no, she thought. *I was thinking about how quickly you climbed out of the toilet-hole.*

"Well, wonder no more. She's dead."

!!!

"That's right. Dead."

It couldn't be true. The killer was lying.

"I saw her in the basement, grabbing a game of Parcheesi down from the shelf in the closet, and I came up behind her, and I sliced her pretty little throat."

"You did?"

"Sure. Now, the question I have for you is, why did you abandon her?"

"Abandon?"

"Did I stutter? Abandon. You sent her down there to what you knew could possibly be her demise, and you just...bolted. Not a very sisterly thing to do. Not honorable at all. And one thing I can't stand..."

The killer grabbed her by her beautiful long blond flowing hair.

"is..."

Her hair was pulled tighter, ever tighter, until she felt her scalp start to tear right from the bone.

"a lack of honor."

The killer let go of her hair before it completely ripped away.

"But the more I thought about it, the more I thought, Hey, maybe she's trying to help me. I don't know why, but maybe she's trying to make it easy on me. It just might pay to have somebody like that on my team."

???

"So the question is now, do I kill you or do I let you live?"

"I vote live," Muffy said.

"I bet you do. But I haven't decided yet. Come with me."

The killer walked with her, a firm grip on her shoulder, back to the house.

"You really stink," she said.

"I just climbed out of a toilet-hole."

46. The Note

Hey, I decided this would be fun. I..."

Buffy's incessant rambling was cut short. Her sister wasn't in the living room.

"Muffy?" she called out to the emptiness around her. No answer.

"Muffy?" she called again, this time a little louder. She still received no reply.

She ran quickly upstairs and into Chet's room.

"Chet, have you seen Muffy?" she asked.

"Yeah, about an hour ago. When we were all sitting on the couch."

"I mean recently, asshole."

"Can't say I have."

She raced across the hallway to Ben's room, and flung open the door. "Ben have you seen...oh." Her face turned away.

"Have I seen who?" he asked, his voice so raspy, his lungs so fluid-filled that she could barely make out his words.

"My sister?" she asked, once again turning to face him, but crossing her eyes as she did so, so all she got was a fuzzy image.

"No, sorry."

"Okay, thanks," she said, and raced down the stairs once again.

That's when she noticed it. She should have seen it all along. The front door had been flung wide open.

Of course. The outhouse.

Not even realizing she still held the game in her hands, she let it drop to the floor, little pieces from Clue spilling out all over the place; a plastic rope here, a plastic candlestick there, Colonel Mustard rolling under the couch, Professor Kumquat rolling underneath Martin Mull, etc.

She headed toward the shitter. That little bitch. She had it planned all along to get her to leave so she could go running into her hiding spot like a little coward. Why, when she saw her, she was gonna tan her hide.

"Muffy?" she yelled, but got no answer.

"Muffy?!?!?!?" she screamed even louder, as you can tell by my use of punctuation.

She flung open the outhouse door. Empty.

Oh, shit. If Muffy wasn't hiding, then the only other possibility was...

And as if to conform her fear, she noticed that tacked to the wall was a piece of paper. And underneath it, a set of keys. She grabbed hold of the paper. It was a note, which she read by the moonlight's glow.

Dear Twin Number Two, it read.

Don't bother looking for her. She's already dead. Found her in the privacy shed. Ha! Anyway, you may notice the keys hanging below. They belong to the van. Please take my advice and leave now, or you may never make it out alive.

Keep it real,

The killer.

And P.S. I believe you are all idiots for not leaving the first day. What is wrong with you people?

That's it! She needed to get out of here now.

She put her grieving for her sister on hold for the time being; she had to think about escape.

She took the key ring off the nail. However, instead of heading directly to the van, she marched back into the house. She knew the killer told her to leave now, but there was no way in hell she was going to leave Ben here. And yes, even Chet deserved a chance to get out, she supposed.

She fled back upstairs and into Ben's room. She made the mistake this time of looking at him directly. She felt her stomach juices rise up into her throat, but she would not throw up this time. She didn't want him to realize just how bad he looked. He wasn't even recognizable any more.

"Ben, we gotta get out of here," she said.

"Out of here? What..."

"We gotta leave. I got the van keys. Chet and I will help get you to the van. We gotta get out. Look."

She handed him the note the killer had left.

It took him a minute to adjust his eyes enough so he could read it, since there wasn't really much left of them.

He closed his eyelids, and shook his head. A tear actually managed to escape, or maybe that was mucus.

"I can't go," he said.

"What?" she asked, incredulous. "What do you mean you can't go?"

"Read the note," he said, his voice becoming less audible the more he spoke. It sounded like he was trying to talk underwater. "It says leave now. I'll only slow you down."

"But you have to go," Buffy said. "I don't care if you slow me down; I'm not leaving without you."

"Listen to me. Buffy. You have to go now. Or you're going to die. Grab Chet and leave. Please."

"Okay, see ya," she said, and jetted out the door. There was no way she was going to convince him, so why bother wasting time?

"Buffy," she heard him say. She headed back.

"Did you ever find the salve?"

"Ben, we've been over this. We've all looked for salve. There's none anywhere. Sorry."

"Okay, take care," he said.

She contemplated not going to get Chet, contemplated hard, but at last, she decided to be a Good Samaritan and do her one good deed for the day.

"We gotta get out of here," she told him.

"What do you mean out of here?" he asked.

"Look," she said, and handed him the note.

He read it. "Huh," he said and shook his head. "We're not going anywhere."

"What?" she said. "Of course we are. Come on, I got the van key."

"No, no, no. Don't you see? It's a trap. The killer's setting you up."

"I don't have time to argue about this. I gotta get the fuck out of here. Now, are you coming or not?"

"Come on, Buffy. You're intelligent. Don't you know a setup when you see one? You get in that van, and the killer will be waiting for you in there. Or you turn the key and a bomb will go off. We've all been dying in very creative ways. Don't you realize this is a setup for the most creative one yet?"

"Fine. Stay here and die," she said, and headed downstairs. A setup? Maybe. But perhaps there was a slim chance that the note was sincere. That the killer indeed wanted to spare her, for some reason.

She looked out the door. The van was over to the left, facing the camp. All she had to do was step outside and walk ten paces or so, open the van door and step inside.

She did just that. And you know what? Nothing bad happened. She checked the back seat for any stowaways, which perhaps she should have done before she got in, but it was too dark to see anything back there from outside anyway. The coast was clear. No one in the van but her. She only prayed it would start.

The slamming door jolted Muffy awake. She dreamt that she was giving some guy with a cold dick a blowjob.

Well, she was giving somebody a blowjob. Was it the killer? That motherfucker was taking advantage of her while she was passed out. That miserable sonofabitch.

But as her senses started to come back to her she realized that wasn't a dick in her mouth. Where was she? What was going on? Was this some sort of vehicle she was under? Oh my God, was this... Was this the van?

She tried removing her mouth from the van's exhaust pipe, but that fucker had glued her lips around it.

The van was shaking over her. Somebody was in there.

She tried to shout. *Wait! Help!* But the majority of her breath went into the tailpipe.

Oh God, oh God, oh God, how was she going to get out of this?

Well, to hell with it; if she had to rip her lips off to get out, she would. She pulled as hard as she could, but her lips didn't tear as easily as she thought they would.

Buffy put the key in the ignition, prayed again silently, and turned it. The van choked and chugged a little, but wouldn't start. Come on, goddammit.

Muffy coughed as she got a lungful of exhaust. Smoke shot from her nose. She tried again to break free. She pulled harder. The pipe was not budging.

"Come on, come on," she said, as she thought of all the horror flicks where the last person tried to leave and the car wouldn't start. This was bullshit. Well, the van wasn't in the best of shape, and being parked there for a week, maybe it just decided to give up.

She turned the key once again. The van choked and sputtered and finally just as it sounded like it wasn't going to happen, the engine turned over, and the van sprung to life. Hooray!

She threw the van into reverse, and turned the wheel sharply to head toward the driveway.

Bump!

What was that she just ran over? That didn't sound good. Did she just lose the muffler or something? Suddenly, this didn't seem right. She knew this was all going way too smoothly. She put the van in park and got out.

She walked around the back and saw what was left of her sister.

She could tell it was her sister from her clothes, but those were the only things that were recognizable, as her face had been crushed like a Gallagher melon under the weight of the van.

"Mufffeeeee!!!" she screamed. She fell to her knees and cradled her sister's dead body. The full magnitude of what she had just done hit her.

She had just killed her own sister.

That motherfucker had set her up. How was she going to live with this, knowing she had just killed her sister?

She heard footsteps approaching. She looked up, and saw.

The killer.

"Congratulations," he (Or was it she? She couldn't tell from the whisper) said. "That's one less that I had to do. Want a job?"

She shook her head. Normally, she would have started fighting, but all the fire had fizzled out of her as she held Muffy's flattened skull.

"Feel terrible, don't you?"

She nodded.

"Want to die?"

She nodded again.

"Thought so,"

And that's when Buffy's lights went out.

47. The Final Chapter

Ben lay there in his steaming pile of self, yellow and green fluids oozing out in all directions. He tried to lift his arm, just to see if it was possible, but the vile slurping sound it made when it tried to free itself from his bed sheet made him want to vomit. It was as though so much of his flesh had melted away that he had become one with the bed. He was no longer human- he was part mattress.

He didn't know what to do. He wanted to get up and run away. Grab the van keys and go- get the fuck out of Dodge. But it was a little too late to think about that. The only thing he could do was lay there and wait to die. Now he knew what it must feel like to get old. Your body deteriorates and becomes useless, yet your mind is still fresh, still clear as a bell. You want to get up and shout and run and skip and jump and fuck and have a blast and change the world, but you can't do shit but lay there in your hospital bed and wait to die. And it was nice that he was getting to experience this feeling now, since he would never make it to old age. At this point, he doubted if he would even make it to Friday.

So, helplessly he lay there. Helplessly he laid there. He tried both sentences out in his mind and decided that the first one was grammatically correct, although the second one sounded right to him.

Helpless, he lay there and listened. He heard it all from his window. Buffy turning the key in the ignition. He heard the van start, and for a moment, he heard it backing up. Then he heard the door slam and the horrifying screams of her sister's name. He heard the pitiful sobbing that soon followed.

And after that, the silence.

And Chet must have heard it, too, although he was clear across the other side of the house. Yes, he must have heard it, because a couple minutes later Ben heard him say, "That's it! I've had it!" and run down the stairs.

Chet! He wanted to scream at him, but his lungs were so full of phlegm and God only knew what else, that all he could do was mouth the word and eke out a soft rattle.

Well, to hell with it. What could he do about it at this point? Their fates were all sealed. Their fates were sealed SIX days ago when they arrived here. No, they were sealed way back when he was planning this trip. He sealed their fates. It was his fault. What the hell was he thinking? That the murders that occurred on Harm's Way would never happen again? My God, he led them all into a death trap. The conditions were right. It had happened before, on this road, with a group of teenagers that were just like them. He thought it was a fun little story to tell them. He thought the fear factor would add to the excitement of it all. Well, how excited are you now, Ben? Lying there in your bed, burnt beyond recognition, while you listen to your last living friend run head-first into certain death? Not a fun little story anymore, is it? Now it's real.

Enough of the blame. He couldn't concentrate on blame over the racket that Chet was making outside.

Chet. Poor bastard. *Maybe he'll pull through,* Ben thought. But he knew it wasn't true. He knew there was no defeating the killer. It was too cunning. It had killed so many times before successfully; there was no way Chet was going to beat it. Oh, how he wished he could stop him.

But the more he thought about it, the more he realized Chet was doing a very brave and noble thing. Although quite stupid, this was probably the only act of noncowardice he had performed in his life. Chet had spent so much of his life running from his problems, running from himself. And if he was going to die (which he was, let's face it), then at least he would die knowing he had tried to avenge the death of his friends. And there was probably no better feeling than that.

"COME ON OUT, YOU SONOFABITCH!" he heard Chet yell.

"REALLY BRAVE, HUH? KILLING PEOPLE IN THEIR SLEEP AND WHEN THEY'RE VULNERABLE! WHY DON'T YOU COME FIGHT ME, ONE ON ONE, HUH?" He was really pushing his luck. Go, Chet!

"COME ON, LET'S GO! OH! OH! I SEE YOU THERE! COME ON OUT! WHAT ARE YOU? SCARED? THAT'S WHAT I THOUGHT! CHICKEN! CHEEP-CHEEP-CHEEEEEP-CHEEEEEEP!

"YEAH, THAT'S RIGHT! COME ON OUT! THERE YOU GO! YOU MOTHERFUCKER, YOU'RE GONNA DIE! YOU'RE GONNA DIE! COME ON! COME..."

And just like that, his shouts were silenced. No screaming. No pleading for his life. He just went out, in a blaze of glory.

Ben wondered if the killer was even going to bother with him. He thought the answer to that question was no. If the killer was as merciless as he thought, he would probably just be left to die on his own.

He was in so much pain right now. There was only one way out, besides waiting it out. For better or worse, he was left in charge of his own life. He couldn't keep on like this.

He wasn't sure where he was getting the strength, and he didn't really care. Finally, after all this time, he was managing to get himself up off the bed. Were the sheets still stuck to him? Sure. Was he leaving a giant trail of mucus behind him? Sure. Was he able to stand up and walk to the bathroom? No. No he wasn't, but he was able to crawl his way there. Crawling. Just a tangle of flesh and bed sheets, crawling, slurrrping its way into the bathroom. He didn't know what he would find in the medicine cabinet, probably a lot of expired shit, but it didn't matter. There had to be something in there he could take to end his life. He looked up at the medicine cabinet from the bathroom floor. God, it was a long way up. There was no way in hell he was ever going to get up there to reach it. He'd have to settle for whatever he could find in the vanity.

Ben felt his strength failing. He was going fast. Maybe there was no need for him to kill himself after all. Maybe if he just waited a few more minutes, the infection would kill him, and it would be over. But he couldn't do it. He couldn't go out like that. He needed to end it. If he just let the infection kill him, it would be like the killer was doing it. No, he'd had his entire vacation ruined by the will of that damaged fuck; it was his turn to control his fate now.

He flung open the door under the sink. Bathroom cleaner! There it was! But was Mr. Clean strong enough? Shit, when he was a little boy he'd gotten into a bottle of bleach and had almost the whole thing guzzled by the time his mother found him. And that didn't kill him, so why would Mr. Clean? He moved it aside to look for something stronger, and there, gleaming like a shining beacon, was a generic Walgreen's tube, with one word printed on the front:

SALVE.

"Here," he gurgled, although nobody would have been able to understand him, were anyone around. "Here it is! Right behind the cleaner." He was fading out. "See?" he said, fading. "All you gotta do is look."

All you gotta do is look.

Dear God,

Ok, I did it! I killed them all. And you thought it couldn't be done. You thought it was too much of a task to rid the earth of that many people in that short a time, especially for someone like myself. But I did it. I did it!

Darkness will reign no more. You needed me to do your bidding. Sure, you may not have asked me directly, but I can tell, dear Lord, that you needed my help. You are far too busy trying to end the wars that are going on, trying to feed the starving children around the world, trying to put a stop to disease and whatnot, so I shall take care of the small things for you.

Do not worry any longer about such petty things. I am the new messiah! Or not. Who knows?

Let me tell you- it wasn't easy. Single-handedly murdering all of those children was a task that couldn't be taken lightly. I couldn't just go in there and start slaughtering one by one. It took cunning. It took skill. It took imagination.

Even the "good" ones, Lord. Even they needed to meet their end. No one is without sin. Least of all, this group of miscreants.

Take that boy Adam, for example. Seemingly such a nice, pure boy. But he harbored a dark secret that could not be overlooked.

The twins, ah the twins. Just goes to prove that trouble comes in twos. Filthy whores. They needed to be cut down.

Even that boy Brent. Very studious, that one. Why would I take down one of your smartest, most promising children? He was evil, too. Look at the games he played. Those fantasy games filled with monsters and demons. Once you start playing with demons, you become one yourself.

Really, do I need to go any further to explain my motives? I believe I do. I may not need to justify my actions to you, but I will always need justification and vindication from myself.

Sometimes, Lord, I feel like I carry a much larger burden than you. I mean, sure, you have the entire world to take care of, whereas I only have a handful here and there, but you have magic powers. I do not. I am only human. Although sometimes, I don't know, I feel, almost supernatural, above humankind. Now, where was I?

Evil comes in many forms, Lord, and drugs are pure evil. That boy Simon, whom the kids call "Jonesy", fell into the evil grasp of drugs. The argument may be made that marijuana, mushrooms, and other drugs were put here by you, in nature, therefore they're all right. I think differently. Take the cannabis plant, for example. A beautiful plant. I believe it was put here by you to look at; you never told us to smoke it. That aside, this boy was using heroin. Heroin! From the beautiful poppy, and tweaked up by mankind to suit his evil need to escape this beautiful world. Pure horror.

Virtue is a heavy load, but I think I wear it well, what say you?

Everyone needs to be comfortable with who they are, because they are who you made them to be. Darnell was trying to be something he was not. He could have grown up to be a nice, upstanding black man, one with integrity, but he chose instead to pretend to be a gangster. If he continued down this path, it would have had dire consequences.

Never in my life have I seen such evil as that Kiera girl. Calling herself "goth". Wearing black makeup. Listening to satanic music. Thinking suicidal thoughts. Nothing she ever did had even a shred of decency. Horrible, horrible girl.

Which leads me to that boy, Floyd. A nice young southern boy. Sang your praises every Sunday morning and read the Bible regularly. But he was not without sin. Alcohol consumption. Gluttony. Laziness. All sins. All punishable.

Oh, and that Chet boy. A nasty, filthy creature. So full of himself he didn't have room for anything else. Promiscuous. Alcoholic. Obnoxious.

Regrets, I've had a few. And I don't really know what that boy Doris' deal was, but I'm sure he was up to no good. They all are, aren't they?

Down to Ben, the one who brought them there. The one who allowed all of this debauchery to take place. I believe he carried the sin of all of them combined. Enough said.

So I guess that's it for now, Lord. I hope I have pleased you once again, and I hope all is well with you. Keep my seat warm for me.

Sincerely,

Want to read more? Go to my web page www.marcrichardauthor.com and sign up to the mailing list to get free books! It only gets better from here, folks.

Please don't forget to leave a review. A man's gotta make a living!

Marc Richard is the author of Those Eyes: A Love Story, Degrees of Separation, It'll End in Tears, Sorry, the DAVE! Series, and the Alphabet Books series.. Read more Marc Richard. You know you want to.

Made in the USA
Coppell, TX
13 July 2021